Date
A Live
Truth Miku

"Kurumi?"

Shido Itsuka
A high school student

"Please, stay still for a moment."

Kurumi
A Spirit

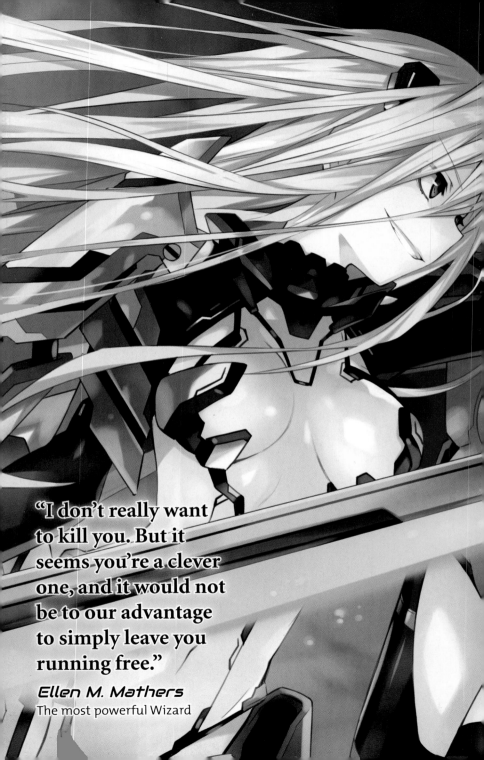

"I don't really want to kill you. But it seems you're a clever one, and it would not be to our advantage to simply leave you running free."

Ellen M. Mathers
The most powerful Wizard

"Hngh..."

Origami Tobiichi
Shido's classmate

"I promised you."

"Huh…?"

Miku
A Spirit

"The kingdom
has inverted.
Now, brace
yourselves,
humanity."

Isaac Westcott
Managing Director
of DEM Industries

CONTENTS

Date A Live
Truth Miku

07

Koushi Tachibana

Illustrated by
Tsunako

YEN
ON

New York

Date A Live
Truth Miku
07

Koushi Tachibana

Translation by Jocelyne Allen
Cover art by Tsunako

This book is a work of fiction. Names, characters, places, and incidents are the product of the author's imagination or are used fictitiously. Any resemblance to actual events, locales, or persons, living or dead, is coincidental.

DATE A LIVE Vol.7 MIKU TRUTH
©Koushi Tachibana, Tsunako 2013
First published in Japan in 2013 by KADOKAWA CORPORATION, Tokyo.
English translation rights arranged with KADOKAWA CORPORATION, Tokyo through TUTTLE-MORI AGENCY, Inc., Tokyo.

English translation © 2022 by Yen Press, LLC

Yen On
150 West 30th Street, 19th Floor
New York, NY 10001

Visit us at yenpress.com
facebook.com/yenpress
twitter.com/yenpress
yenpress.tumblr.com
instagram.com/yenpress

First Yen On Edition: October 2022
Edited by Yen On Editorial: Ivan Liang
Designed by Yen Press Design: Andy Swist

Yen On is an imprint of Yen Press, LLC.
The Yen On name and logo are trademarks of Yen Press, LLC.

The publisher is not responsible for websites (or their content) that are not owned
 by the publisher.

Library of Congress Cataloging-in-Publication Data
Names: Tachibana, Koushi, 1986– author. | Tsunako, illustrator. | Allen, Jocelyne, 1974– translator.
Title: Date a live / Koushi Tachibana ; illustration by Tsunako ; translation by Jocelyne Allen.
Other titles: Dēto a raibu. English
Description: First Yen On edition. | New York, NY : Yen On, 2021–
Identifiers: LCCN 2020054696 | ISBN 9781975319915 (v. 1 ; trade paperback) |
    ISBN 9781975319939 (v. 2 ; trade paperback) | ISBN 9781975319953 (v. 3 ; trade paperback) |
    ISBN 9781975319977 (v. 4 ; trade paperback) | ISBN 9781975319991 (v. 5 ; trade paperback) |
    ISBN 9781975320010 (v. 6 ; trade paperback) | ISBN 9781975348298 (v. 7 ; trade paperback)
Subjects: GSAFD: Science fiction. | Fantasy fiction.
Classification: LCC PL876.A23 D4813 2021 | DDC 895.63/6—dc23
LC record available at https://lccn.loc.gov/2020054696

ISBNs: 978-1-9753-4829-8 (paperback)
        978-1-9753-4830-4 (ebook)

1 2022

LSC-C

Printed in the United States of America

Spirit

A uniquely catastrophic creature existing in a parallel world. Cause of occurrence and reason for existence unknown. Creates a spacequake and inflicts serious damage on her surroundings whenever she appears in this world. A very powerful fighter.

Strategy No. 1

Annihilate with force. This approach is very difficult, since the Spirit is extremely powerful, as noted above.

Strategy No. 2

...Date her and make her all weak in the knees.

Truth Miku

Spirit No. 10
Astral Dress—Princess Type
Weapon—Throne Type [Nahemah]

Chapter 6
Nightmare, Redux

"You seem to be in a bit of trouble, Shido. Say, maybe we could chat for a second?" the girl said, smiling bewitchingly as she crawled out of the inky shadows in the dark abandoned building.

"Wha…" Shido couldn't even cry out as his eyes grew wide in surprise and confusion. He simply stared at this strange sight.

The girl was so gorgeous, a shiver ran up his spine.

But anyone who had come face-to-face with this particular girl would immediately understand that his reaction was not simply because of her otherworldly beauty. There was no hint of affection or delight in the smile that stretched across her face, only the absolute confidence of a natural predator and an aura that made the skin crawl.

Her jet-black hair was tied back in asymmetrical braids, which swung each time she giggled. A dress the color of blood and shadow coiled around her slender body. But her most unusual feature was undoubtedly her eyes. Two different colors set in her beautiful face. A close look revealed the face of a clock in her left eye, complete with hands that marked the passage of time with a steady *tic-tic-tic*.

"Kurumi Tokisaki?!" Shido squeezed the girl's name out of his throat.

She was his former classmate and the most malicious of Spirits, one who killed people of her own volition.

Her eyebrows jumped up, and she shrugged slightly. "Oh dear. Was

I mistaken? Yoshino and the Yamai sisters stolen by a Spirit, Tohka abducted by DEM… You certainly seem like you're at the end of your rope and without a single card left to play."

"You—," he gasped.

Everything she said was exactly right.

A few hours earlier in Tengu Square, the venue for the Tenou Festival, he had faced off against Miku Izayoi, a Spirit who controlled sound and voice. Through her Angel Gabriel, Miku had gained total control over Yoshino, Kaguya, Yuzuru, and all the spectators in the venue.

On top of that, Kotori and her crew had also turned on him, after hearing a certain sound through the speakers, no doubt. And right when things seemed like they couldn't get any worse, DEM Wizard Ellen burst onto the scene and made off with Tohka.

Although Shido had just barely made it out in one piece and managed to hide himself in an abandoned building on the outskirts of town, there was nothing he could actually do about the situation except pound his fists against the floor in frustration over his own helplessness.

Kurumi was 100 percent correct. But that was exactly why he didn't get what she wanted to chat about.

"How'd you know all that?" he asked warily.

"Hee-hee-hee! Do you mind not asking such inconsiderate questions? When it comes to you, Shido, I know everything there is to know. Obviously," Kurumi said, smiling adorably.

For some reason, the shadow at her feet squirmed, and he felt like he could hear any number of tiny voices laughing.

"…"

He gulped loudly, remembering the scene he'd witnessed a few months earlier. It was no exaggeration to say that Kurumi did have more than the usual number of eyes and ears. It wouldn't surprise him at all if one or two of her avatars had been in the venue earlier.

A loud alarm began to sound inside his head.

Kurumi knew that there was absolutely nothing protecting him right now. No one would come running. No one would interfere with her *meal*.

"Ngh..." Shido stiffened and stepped back.

Kurumi stretched her lips out cheerily. "Hee-hee! Please, calm yourself. For the moment, at least, I have no intention of doing anything to you."

"What?" He furrowed his brow at this. "What do you mean? I thought your goal was to eat me or whatever?"

"Yes, I won't deny that." She nodded neatly. "But weren't you listening? I said I wished to speak with you."

"...And you're saying I should just trust you?"

"There's no reason for me to lie right now, is there?"

"Mm." Shido drew his lips into a tight line.

She was right. Given the current situation, Kurumi could kill or eat him whenever she felt like it. He couldn't think of any explanation for her to go out of her way to lie to someone whose life she held in her hands. Although when it came to this particular girl, there was a chance she might just want to see his face relax in relief right before she terrorized him once more. That might have been all this was.

Shido realized it was pointless to worry, but he still didn't let down his guard as he glared back at her. "What exactly do we have to talk about?"

"What's going to happen next, of course."

"And what's that supposed mean?" he asked dubiously.

Kurumi walked over to him, her heels clacking rhythmically on the floor. She leaned in close, brought her mouth to his ear, and whispered, "Say, Shido? Wouldn't you like to rescue Tohka?"

"What?" he asked reflexively, doubting his own ears. "What do you mean?"

"Exactly what I said," she replied primly. "Wouldn't you like to save Tohka from DEM Industries?"

"O-of course I would! That company wants to kill Spirits!" he cried. "I can't let them keep Tohka prisoner!"

"Kee-hee-hee!" Kurumi laughed with delight. "I suppose not, hm? I suppose not. That is just how you are."

Shido scowled, a vague uneasiness creeping up on him. "But why are you even asking?"

"Kee-hee-hee! Hee-hee!" Kurumi licked his ear, still wearing that bewitching smile.

"...!"

"You want to save Tohka," she continued. "But no matter how much you pray, it's impossible for you to do alone, yes? For starters, you don't even know where they've taken her. And even if you did pin down the location, I have to imagine that the DEM have fortified their defenses after getting a hold of their precious Spirit. And we haven't even touched upon that Wizard who abducted Tohka in the first place. *That woman* is trouble. She's far too much for any regular human being to contend with."

"You don't need to tell me that!" he cried. "I know I don't stand a chance! But I still have to—"

"Yes, yes. I suppose you would say that, Shido," Kurumi cut him off, nodding. "That's not an act of courage, but folly. You can't make things happen just because you have *feelings*. If you try this all by yourself, you'll either be killed or taken captive."

"Ngh." He gritted his teeth. "So what then?"

"Hee-hee-hee!" She giggled again. "Don't you see? I'm saying that I'm generously offering to assist you."

"Wha...?!" His eyes flew open at the impossible words coming out of Kurumi's mouth. "Help? You? Me?"

"Yes. I shall lend you my aid in liberating Tohka," she confirmed with a grin.

Unable to grasp exactly what Kurumi was up to, Shido put a hand to his forehead in an attempt to calm his chaotic thoughts.

Kurumi was a Spirit—and one equipped with the most powerful Angel he'd ever seen. If he had her help, he would have a shot at the nearly impossible objective of saving Tohka.

But he still couldn't accept the proposal at face value.

"What's your game?" he demanded to know.

"Oh, honestly!" She waved her hands theatrically. "I simply wish to be of use to you, Shido."

There was no chance she genuinely thought he would believe that without reserve.

"You..." Shido rolled his eyes at her.

"Oh dear, oh my, oh no." Kurumi brought her hands up to her eyes and wiped at them as if she were weeping pitifully. "That makes me so sad. I am only thinking of *you*."

"…" He continued to give her a dubious stare.

"You don't trust me, hm? Well, I suppose that's only to be expected." Kurumi shrugged, as if she'd gotten tired of her own act. "If I were to confess a truth, I have business with DEM Industries on another matter. I help you, you act as bait, Shido. A little give-and-take."

"Business?" He frowned.

"Yes, I'm searching for a particular person."

"Who exactly?"

"That is a secret." Kurumi held a finger up to her lips and winked. "Please don't fret. I have told you no lies. But, of course, if you still don't believe me, I won't force the issue."

"Unh…" His throat tightened.

He couldn't trust Kurumi. That was true. But it was also true that she was his only option. Did the glass in front of him now contain poison or medicine? He had no idea, but his current ailment would kill him if he sat here and did nothing.

He had no choice but to pick up the glass, even if it meant taking a risk. Even if it was poison, he would have to drink deeply if he wanted to save Tohka.

"Fine. I believe you. Please, help me, Kurumi!" Shido said, clenching his hands into fists.

Kurumi pinched her skirt and bent at the knees to offer a graceful curtsy. "I would be delighted to." She acted just like the sheltered daughter of a wealthy family, bowing playfully as she giggled.

Then she whirled around, the hem of her skirt flipping up, and took a few dancing steps before turning back to Shido.

"Now then! Shall we get started? There is no time for dallying. Some say haste makes waste, but that just means we need to wrap this up before that happens."

"Yeah." Shido nodded. "So what should I do? I'll do whatever it takes to save Tohka."

Kurumi's smile grew even broader. "Oh, yes, yes. Wonderful Tohka.

How lucky she is to have someone who cares so much for her! Hee-hee-hee! I'm so jealous."

"D-don't tease me."

"I'm not teasing you at all. But unfortunately, I can't do anything about that yet. *We* are still confirming Tohka's location. Might I have just a little more time?"

"...You came prepared."

"Hee-hee-hee!" She giggled wildly. "Well, there was no possibility of you rejecting this plan."

"Ngh..." Shido screwed up his face bitterly. He felt as if he were being led around by the nose. "B-but then we can't do anything yet."

"That's not the case at all," she said quickly, almost interrupting him. "Before we rush to the rescue of our dear Tohka, there is a little something we must take care of, yes?"

He quickly guessed what she was getting at. With a heavy sigh, he said, "Miku?"

Kurumi nodded. "That was indeed the name, wasn't it? Of that wonderful songstress."

The main reason Shido was hiding in an abandoned building on the outskirts of town was none other than the fact that he was under attack by the Spirit Miku Izayoi.

Using voice and sound to control people, Miku had amassed a terrifying number of troops, and her army left no stone unturned in their search for Shido. To make him pay for betraying her.

Shido grew grim when he was reminded of this, and Kurumi grinned abruptly, as if she had just remembered something.

"What?" he demanded.

"Oh no, I was merely thinking about the performance today," she replied. "Hee-hee-hee! You looked wonderful, Shido. Or should I say, *Shiori?*"

"...Hngh." Shido scowled and averted his eyes.

In order to butter up the man-hating Miku, he'd been forced to dress up as a girl, and Kurumi had apparently spotted him.

"Well, whatever the reason, this Miku is in a frenzy. She's very invested in catching you. Not to mention the tens of thousands of people and the three Spirits following this general's orders... Would you consider that an accurate description of the current situation?"

"...Yeah, that's right."

"Hmm." She tapped her chin with a finger. "Well then, how about we take care of her first? Slowly but surely, she is expanding the area under her control. If this keeps up, we may even be interrupted before we can mount our heroic rescue of dear Tohka. And I would be inconvenienced as well if you wound up captured by her, Shido."

"'Take care of her'?" He raised an eyebrow. "You say that like it's so simple, but..."

"It's actually not all that difficult. From what I've observed, she doesn't appear to have any power suited for actual combat."

"Maybe not, but she has an Angel and a voice that can control people."

"That won't be a problem. I am not so pure and innocent as to be swayed by such a performance. Leave her to me. I'll make it a clean kill," Kurumi said jokingly as she raised her index finger and thumb to fire an imaginary gun. *Bang!*

Shido hurriedly shook his head. "N-no! You can't!"

"Hee-hee-hee! It was merely a joke. If nothing else, I do understand that gentle Shido would never agree with such a resolution. After all, you are an eccentric who would even try to save *me*." Kurumi smiled again. But for some reason, he felt like her expression now was slightly different from her previous cheery grins.

But before he could comment on this, Kurumi continued.

"But it is a teensy bit of a bother not to have such means at my disposal. And since we may not be able to convince her to pull back, given the short amount of time we have, we must at the very least make her promise not to touch you until we have rescued Tohka."

"Promise?" Shido scratched his head, a complicated look on his face. It was true that he couldn't leave things as they were and allow Miku to do more damage. He had to make it happen one way or another. "But how exactly are we going to negotiate with her?"

The issue was that army of hers. A wall of people guarded Miku. He didn't even know how large their ranks would swell. It would be nigh impossible to even get close to her.

Perhaps guessing at Shido's thoughts, Kurumi put a hand to her chin. "What if we could get Miku and you alone together?"

"Huh? Well, yeah, if we could do that...," he started, and then shook his head. "No. It'd be tough. You may have noticed she's not the kind of person you can talk to. Especially since she seriously hates my guts. And anyway, her views on human beings are totally warped. Maybe because she was born a Spirit with a voice that can control people."

Kurumi arched an eyebrow dubiously.

"What is it, Kurumi?" he asked.

"I do wonder about that," she replied, finger pressed thoughtfully to her chin.

"Huh?" Shido cocked his head to one side.

Kurumi rolled her eyes. "I don't quite know how to explain it. But was she really *born* with those values?"

"What do you mean?"

"Oh, how can I put it? She seems the tiniest bit off." Kurumi frowned. A second later, she lifted her face like she had just thought of something. "Shido. Would we be able to obtain something that belongs to Miku?"

"Like...her stuff? Why?"

"If my instincts are correct, we may be able to pin down her weak point."

"What?!" Shido frowned dubiously.

Kurumi didn't seem to be trying to deceive him. He had no idea what her plan could possibly be, but she clearly had something in mind. And although he had no solid reason to have faith in her, given that his back was pressed up against a wall, he had no choice but to grab on to whatever looked like it would keep him afloat.

That said, they were talking about a Spirit here. The idea that they could just get their hands on Miku's belongings was too...

"Actually, wait." His cheek twitched, and he put a hand to his chin.

"Nn… Unh…" Tohka opened her eyes with a quiet moan and yawned. "Haaah."

This was how she woke up every morning. In her sleepy mind, Tohka walked through her routine.

First, she would open her eyes. Then she'd get out of bed and wash her face. After that, eat breakfast, get dressed…and yes, she'd go to school with Shido. Today's lunch would probably be his special bento. What would he put in it today? Her heart danced in her chest at the mere thought of it.

"Mm… Hmm."

Dozing and drowsing, she tried to climb out of bed. Which was when Tohka realized she couldn't actually move.

"Mm?" She tried to rub her bleary eyes and take a look at her surroundings, but she couldn't lift her hand up.

Frowning, she looked down and discovered that she was sitting in a metal chair with sturdy cuffs around her wrists and ankles. There was also an IV needle in her arm, and several electrodes were stuck to her head and limbs.

"What…is this…"

She looked closer and saw that she was not wearing her usual pajamas, either. Perhaps she had changed at some point—she was now dressed in her Raizen High School uniform.

Tohka twisted her head to look around.

She wasn't in her room. Or at Shido's house. This place was completely unknown to her, about the same size as her high school classroom. She could see what looked to be a camera and a speaker in one corner, but there was nothing else in the room—just hard floor and walls. Plus, she couldn't see anything resembling a door, much less a window.

It was a strange space. If forced to describe it, she would have said it somehow felt similar to the solitary confinement cell she had seen on TV a while ago, the one where they put all the really bad prisoners.

"Where...am I?" She blinked rapidly, woke up fully, and set her brain to work.

A few moments later, she finally remembered what had happened before she lost consciousness.

"Right... I was onstage at the Tenou Festival."

In the middle of a fight with the Spirit Miku, who had manifested her Angel and was controlling Yoshino as well as the Yamai sisters, a Wizard clad in platinum armor had appeared. Tohka had managed to get Shido out of harm's way, but she'd ended up losing against the Wizard and had been knocked unconscious.

"So then that means that this is—," she started, then heard a sudden noise in front of her and jerked her head up.

A crack in the shape of a rectangle appeared on the wall where there had been nothing only a moment ago, and the wall slid to the side like a door. A hazy square of light popped up in the gloomy space, and she got a glimpse of the world outside.

And then someone stepped through the door into the room. Pale skin and a bundle of almost white hair stood in sharp contrast to her expensive black suit.

Ellen Mathers. The Wizard who Tohka had crossed swords with at the festival.

"You!" Tohka was ready to leap at Ellen the moment she saw her face. But the metal rings that bound her limbs were strong and didn't so much as flex.

"Please calm down, Tohka. You cannot break those cuffs with the power you have now," Ellen said placatingly.

This effortlessly cool attitude only infuriated Tohka further.

"Don't give me that! What exactly do you want?! Get these off me now!"

"And what would you do if I took them off?"

"Obviously! I'm going to help Shido!" Tohka shouted. She didn't know how much time had passed since the fight at the festival, but she was sure that Shido was on his own and on the run from Miku's forces right about now.

"Shido..." Ellen let out a short sigh. "You mean Shido Itsuka? Please rest assured. We are currently searching for his whereabouts. At the latest, he will be here in a few days."

"Wha...!"

"We are also putting together a siege team for Tengu Square. When dawn breaks, we will launch an all-out assault and apprehend Diva, Hermit, and Berserk. We will bring you face-to-face with your compatriots once more soon enough."

"Y-you brute!" Tohka shouted. "What are you going to do to Shido?!"

"Do not be concerned. We have no intention of being violent with him. Although in the event that he resists, we may have to break an arm or a leg."

"...!" Tohka felt something like fireworks going off inside her head as an unfathomable rage and hatred welled up inside her. The cuffs that had proven entirely unmovable thus far squeaked.

However.

"Wha—?!" She gasped.

Ellen raised an eyebrow ever so slightly, and Tohka's body was pushed back by an invisible force.

"Wh-what is this?!"

It was as if the gravity pushing down on her body had multiplied many times over. Tohka groaned in anguish.

She'd felt this before. It was almost like what she'd experienced when she'd gotten close to Origami and the other AST members. But the strength or maybe the density of it was an order of magnitude greater. Her body felt so heavy that even breathing became difficult. Her consciousness was fading.

"I assume you understand now?" Ellen said, letting out a short breath.

The gravity that had been bearing down on Tohka disappeared as if it had never been in the first place. Air flowed into lungs that had been on the verge of running out of oxygen, and she coughed.

"Kah! Agh!"

"Of all the Wizards, my Territory precision is the greatest. Please understand that there is no point in resisting."

"Ngh." Tohka glared hatefully at Ellen before trying to flex her arms again. But she sensed Ellen's eyes narrowing sharply and gritted her teeth.

With her Spirit power sealed the way it was now, there was no way for her to challenge Ellen's Territory. Tohka clenched her fists in irritation as she stared at Ellen with hard eyes, in an act of the smallest resistance.

"Now then, allow me to ask you a few questions." Ellen pulled out part of the wall to create a simple chair and sat down.

The first thing Origami saw was the color white.

Her mind felt as if it were being yanked back up after sinking deep into a basin of cloudy water as she quickly realized this color was actually a type of building material, and then finally, she noticed that she was lying down.

"Ah…"

It took another few seconds before she could produce a sound. She slowly lifted her arm and found that this was also the color white. It was wrapped in so many bandages, she couldn't see skin.

"O-Origami?!"

She heard a familiar voice and turned her head to find a small girl with her hair tied up in two bundles immediately beside the bed where she lay. A junior member of the SDF Anti-Spirit Team—AST—Mikie Okamine. Her face was decorated with tears and snot; she was a sorry sight.

"Th-thang gooddess… I don't mnow what I bould do if you didn wake ub…"

"Where am I?" Origami asked quietly as she looked at the other girl.

Nose red, Mikie blew her nose with a tissue from a nearby box before replying. "Th-the hospital! Origami, you're really beat up. And you had blood coming out of your eyes and your nose and your ears… I-I didn't know if you'd eber wage ub…"

Her voice got even more incomprehensible toward the end. She pulled out another tissue and blew her nose once more.

"I'm sorry. I'm so sorry… I know you were in danger, but I couldn't do anything. If I had just brushed off the captain and come running, this would never…!" Mikie cried, her face twisting up in regret.

But Origami shook her head as if to reject this. "No need to apologize."

"Huh?" Mikie's eyes grew wide.

"Whatever my reasons, my actions were a complete violation of orders. It had to be a single member going off mission, rather than a concerted action on the part of the AST. Where is Captain Kusakabe?"

"Uh. Um. At the base. She said she was going to discuss your situation with the brass."

"Oh." Origami nodded quietly. But Mikie frowned. She had apparently not yet accepted this.

"B-but, then, you'll…"

"Captain Kusakabe's judgment is correct. If she had helped me, the entire AST might have faced sanctions."

"N-no, but—"

"It's entirely possible. So I'm responsible for this. For taking White Licorice without permission, for attacking Squad Three, all of it is my—"

Her hazy memory suddenly came back clear as day at her own words.

"…!"

Origami's eyes flew open, and she sat up.

No. To be more precise, she *tried* to sit up. The moment she tried, she was struck by a pain so agonizing, it felt as if her bones were crumbling and her muscles snapping.

"Ngh… Unh."

"N-no, Origami! You have to rest!"

"Where's Shido?"

"Huh?"

"Is Shido safe?" Origami asked.

Mikie gasped and then fell silent, apparently considering whether or not she should tell Origami what she knew.

"That's currently being investigated," she said finally. "I don't know the details."

Origami frowned. "Meaning?"

Mikie looked at her with concern before timidly reaching for the remote control and turning the TV on. Video filled the screen; sound came from the speakers.

A news program. She saw a view of the city and heard the panicked voice of a reporter, which no doubt stirred up the anxiety of the average viewer.

"The sudden outbreak of widespread rioting in Tengu City shows no signs of subsiding! Police came to put an end to the violence, and instead joined the rioters! I've never seen anything like this before! What is happening in Tengu?!"

Origami watched the program from where she lay in bed, and a hint of fear colored her face.

"…! This…!"

"It's just how it looks on TV," Mikie said. "The whole city's in chaos. We're not too close to the city, so we're more or less safe here, but…"

"What happened?" Origami asked, stunned.

"It hasn't been made public, but…it's a Spirit," Mikie told her. "We observed a powerful Spirit signal at Tengu Square. We think all those people are being controlled by the Spirit."

"A Spirit… So then why aren't you and the team mobilizing?"

"This is the first time anyone's seen this happen, so the brass is all turned upside down. So far we've been given the order to stand by. I should actually be at the base, but the captain gave me special permission…" Mikie trailed off.

Origami frowned ever so slightly, and that was maybe no wonder.

Whatever else, thousands—or worse, tens of thousands—of people were being controlled by a Spirit. Given how their senior officers wanted to overlook DEM's evildoings, it would have been hard for them to take responsibility and give the order to attack without considering how this would affect DEM.

But with all this going on, what exactly had happened to Shido? Was he under the control of the Spirit like the crowd on the TV? Or…

And then Origami remembered the face of the girl she'd seen before she passed out.

"Mana…"

Former DEM Wizard and Shido's long-lost little sister, Mana Takamiya had saved Origami from that tight spot. She must have also rescued Shido.

"Where's Mana?"

"Mana?" Mikie frowned. "Oh, that's right. I was surprised! I heard no one knew where she went. But then Mana herself came flying up with you in her arms! She was wearing a CR unit I've never seen before, and she said something like, the next time she saw us, she'd probably be our business rival. And then she just jetted off somewhere…"

Origami combed through her memories and recalled the words she'd heard Mana say while she was barely clinging to consciousness. She felt like Mana had indeed said something like that. She didn't know the details, but it seemed certain that she had absconded from DEM at least.

"Nothing about Shido?" she asked.

"N-no." Mikie shook her head. "Unfortunately."

"…Ngh." Origami grunted in vexation and slowly sat up, being careful this time not to place undue burden on any particular part. But even this movement caused her body to shriek. It was badly battered after too many punishing attacks and her own insistence on pushing past her activation limit with that destructive equipment.

"I…have to…" She clenched her fists and beat the bed.

Fwm. A puff of dust rose up.

Origami felt helpless. In the end, she hadn't been able to protect Shido. She had flouted the rules and taken White Licorice, and she still hadn't been able to achieve her objective.

"Shi…do…" She called the name of her lover, wondering if he was okay, and her fists shook.

"This…is it?"

"Yeah. No mistake."

The time was nine PM. Shido and Kurumi were standing in a quiet residential area where the streetlamps and the houses emitted a hazy, warm light. Before them was a tall, elaborate iron fence and a carefully tended yard. And a Western-style house like something out of a fairy tale.

Shido had visited this place just once before—Miku Izayoi's house.

There was likely no one inside. The windows were dark, and the whole place was enveloped in silence.

Investigating the Spirits was extremely difficult since they appeared and disappeared from this world at random. The Spirit known as Miku Izayoi, however, was an exception.

Not only had she been going to school in this world for at least the last several months, but Miku was also a singer who made public appearances. Unlike other Spirits, she had left plenty of traces of herself in this world.

"Well then. Shall we begin our investigation?" Kurumi asked as she raised her right hand.

An old-fashioned pistol jumped out of the shadows into her open palm. And then, without a moment's hesitation, she pulled the trigger. The noise echoed through the night air, and the lock on the gate was blown away.

"Whoa, Kurumi!" Shido cried.

"Is something the matter?" Kurumi cocked her head to one side. "You couldn't possibly be thinking about telling me to stop being so violent, right?"

"No." He paused. "Well, there's that. But think about it. Firing a gun in a quiet neighborhood like this, someone might call the police!"

"But the members of the police force are currently overwhelmed dealing with the riots and are hardly in a position to respond." Kurumi giggled and opened the gate, which creaked laboriously. Ignoring Shido's warning, she fired another shadow bullet at the lock of the front door.

The moment its role was fulfilled, she released the gun, and it was swallowed up by the shadows once more.

"Argh... Unbelievable." Shido scratched at his head and looked both ways to check that there was no one else around before following Kurumi into the house.

"Umm, probably around here." He groped for the light switch, and the chandelier glowed with a gentle light.

Everything inside looked expensive. Although he'd been there once before, he was still overwhelmed.

But now was not the time to be awestruck by the display of material wealth. He flexed all his muscles to psych himself up and then took off his shoes before continuing inside.

"Now then. Where to begin our search?" Kurumi asked.

"Mm. Right." If he was being honest, Shido didn't have any real idea. This was the kind of situation where he wanted to pore over every little nook and cranny, but they couldn't afford such a leisurely search. He recalled the last time he'd been invited to this house.

"The salon on the first floor doesn't really have much of note," he said. "If there's going to be anything, it'll be in Miku's bedroom or something. Maybe."

"I see." Kurumi nodded. "Well, shall we go then?"

"Yeah." He followed her up the stairs.

They found Miku's bedroom soon enough. Once they'd reached the second floor and started down the hallway, they came across a door with a sign that said BEDROOM on it.

"..."

He felt the tiniest bit nervous at the immoral act of entering a girl's bedroom while the owner was out. But he quickly turned that thought into *I'm an idiot thinking about stuff like that at a time like this* and opened the door.

It was maybe thirty square meters, a king-sized bed with a canopy set toward the back while a wooden wardrobe and cabinets lined the walls. And in front of the bed was an enormous TV, likely eighty inches. It was almost like a hotel room.

"This is... Whoa."

He smiled awkwardly without really meaning to. But he couldn't just stand here being surprised. He offered up a quiet "excuse me" as a gesture of remorse before finally entering the room.

The wardrobe and cabinets were straight out of an antique shop, and he opened them up in turn to peek around inside. He mostly found accessories and cute little trinkets. Kurumi wanted something that belonged to Miku. Would this sort of thing work?

"Shido! Shido! Please come and look at this."

He was staring at the accessories with a serious expression on his face when Kurumi called out to him from behind.

"What's up?" he asked. "Did you find something?"

"Yes. I've found something remarkable." She pointed to a drawer in the wardrobe.

He stepped over and turned his eyes where Kurumi's finger was pointing. When he saw what was there, he briefly froze in place.

"Whu..."

The drawer was stuffed full of cute bras and panties.

"See? Do take a look. What an impressive size. I'm certain I could fit my whole head in here." Kurumi picked up a pale bra and held it up with both hands for him to see. And he did see. It really was impressively large. A small watermelon might even fit quite neatly in each cup.

Shido was a healthy boy. So it wasn't that he had no interest in such an appealing item, but right now, the situation was rather pressing. Blushing, he cleared his throat.

"Wh-what are you doing...? Now's not the time for that."

"Hee-hee-hee! You are so deadly serious, Shido. You really must loosen up a teensy bit."

Giggling at her own silliness, Kurumi held the bra up to her own chest. Even though it was on top of her clothes, there was still room to spare in the bra. "Oh my! Oh dear!" she cried.

"...Ungh." Shido felt his face naturally heat up. He hurriedly turned his eyes away.

But it seemed that Kurumi was only too well aware of what was going through his head. She held the bra out to him, seemingly enjoying his reactions.

"Come now, Shido. Won't you try it on as well?"

"H-huh?! Wh-why would I..."

"Oh dear, please excuse me. That was rude." She frowned. "*Shiori*, would you like to?"

"...Ngh." Shido grunted, extraordinary embarrassment coloring his cheeks.

Kurumi smiled bewitchingly as she continued. "I did see you there on the stage from a distance. But I haven't had the opportunity to see Shiori from up close. I do wish to feast my eyes at least once."

"Qu-quit fooling around. I've had enough...!"

Unconsciously, Shido stepped back. But Kurumi pushed forward to close the gap between them.

"I simply do not understand why you find your alter ego so distasteful," she said. "It's not as though it costs you anything."

"It does! Absolutely!" he said. "Specifically time and my dignity!"

"Come now, don't be so cold. It's all right for a just little while, hm? Let me see Shiori's adorable, lovely face trembling in shame just once."

"What are you up to?! Don't go doing anything weird to Shiori!"

"It will be absolutely fine. Absolutely fine."

When Kurumi came even closer, she tripped on the thick rug spread out on the floor, abruptly lost her balance, and toppled forward.

"Oh dear!"

"Wh-whoa!"

She fell in a very deliberate manner to impose her weight on Shido, and he tumbled with her to the ground. On top of that, in a turn of bad luck, they were tangled up in the shelves of the cabinet directly behind them.

There was a terrific clattering and cracking, and he felt an intense pain in the back of his head and along his spine.

"Owowowow." He scowled where he lay flat on his back. "Y-you okay, Kurumi?"

"Yes. I'm quite all right. You were kind enough to save me, Shido."

Kurumi smiled suggestively from where she had fallen onto his chest and pressed her weight up against him unnecessarily.

His shoulders jumped up at the warm pressure of her slender, soft body. "H-hey, Kurumi…"

"Oh my, Shido." Kurumi raised an eyebrow and looked into his face. "You've been injured."

"Huh? Oh, you're right." He touched his cheek and winced. He could feel a little blood there. He must have gotten caught on something when he fell. "I'm okay. This is nothing. Rub a little spit on it and it'll be fine in no time."

"Hmm. Is that so?"

"Yeah. Hurry and get off me already," he said, and tried to sit up again.

But for some reason, Kurumi pressed even harder against him and kept him where he was.

"Kurumi?"

"Please, stay still for a moment."

She spread her legs to straddle his body like a horse, pushed his shoulders down with both hands, and slowly brought her face toward his.

"Wh-what are you doing?!" Shido shrieked, and Kurumi giggled. Her soft breath tickled his ear and nose, and his heart leaped up in his chest.

When he froze in his nervousness, she slowly parted her soft lips, and the tip of her moist tongue peeked out. She pulled her tongue along the cut on his cheek. He felt something indescribable radiate out through his body, making his consciousness flicker.

"Wh-wh-wh-wh-what are you…"

"Hee-hee-hee!" She giggled. "You said it would be fine with a little spit rubbed onto it?"

"N-no, I mean, that's just a figure of speech…," Shido said, and Kurumi chuckled again.

She licked his cheek once more before finally pulling her face away. The string of saliva that stretched out from the tip of her tongue to his cheek glistened in the light. Looking at this excessively obscene sight, he felt his face grow hot again.

Smiling, Kurumi got off him at last. He waited until he had gotten his ragged breathing under control again before sitting up and shaking his head in exasperation.

When he looked back, he saw that the door of the cabinet was indeed seriously banged up. There was no doubt that this would cost money to fix.

"Crap. I didn't want to leave any trace that we were here..."

And then.

"Hm?"

Perhaps it had fallen from the shelf in the impact. He noticed a square tin that hadn't been there when he looked before, and he furrowed his eyebrows slightly.

It was a small container, the kind that usually holds cookies. He knew cookie tins like that were often used to hold random odds and ends, but it felt out of place in this elegant space.

"What's this?"

Curious, he opened it, and his eyes grew round with surprise.

It held a number of plastic CD cases, all of them with Miku on the cover. They appeared to be CDs Miku had released.

"She's got this many songs? ...Wait." Shido unconsciously cocked his head to one side.

The name inscribed below the song titles wasn't Miku's.

"Tsukino Yoimachi? What's with this name?"

For a moment, he thought it was a stage name, but Tonomachi and everyone else had called her Miku Izayoi like normal. There was no doubt that she performed under the name Miku.

And Miku was supposed to be a mysterious idol who performed only at secret live shows limited to female fans. This was the first he'd heard of her proudly gracing the covers of CD jackets like this.

"What is this?" he muttered.

"Is something the matter?" Kurumi peered over his shoulder.

"Mm. Uh-huh," he replied vaguely as he took one of the CDs out of its case, set it in the tray of the nearby CD player, and hit play. Cute upbeat music came out through the speakers, accompanied by Miku's voice.

"Oh my, oh my. What an adorable little song," Kurumi said, waving a finger to the rhythm.

But the vocals sounded just the slightest bit off to Shido.

"This is Miku's voice...isn't it?"

Naturally, there was a difference between live singing and a recording. But it was more than that. This voice was younger—it didn't have the same bewitching appeal that rocked the brain stem the way Miku's voice did now.

The song was filled instead with an earnest determination and a strange charm that animated the listener.

"Hmm."

Although he thought this was suspect, he honestly didn't know what to make of it. He flipped through the CDs in the tin one after another.

"Huh? What's this?" He found something at the very bottom. "A picture?"

Yes. A single photograph in a beautifully decorated frame.

Nothing about that was in and of itself out of the ordinary. However.

"Huh?" He felt a curious sensation graze the back of his mind, and he opened his eyes wide.

Weird. Something is definitely weird.

He picked up the photo again and stared hard at it.

There was no critical bit of information written on the back of the picture. Nor had it been photoshopped in any obvious way. It was an utterly normal photograph.

But that wasn't why he paused. When he really thought about it, this photo shouldn't have existed.

"No way. This is...," he murmured, frowning.

He put a hand to his forehead as his thoughts raced and landed on a certain possibility. It was a possibility that Kotori had rejected. But if he was right, it would explain the existence of this photograph and the CDs he'd found.

"But if that's it, then how…"

As Shido stared at the picture, a pale hand reached out from his side and plucked it from his fingers. He didn't have to wonder who the culprit was—Kurumi.

"This seems to be quite interesting, hm? Allow me to borrow it for a moment."

She held the photo with one of the CDs on top in one hand and threw her free hand up into the air. An old-fashioned pistol appeared from her shadow and settled into her palm.

"Zafkiel. Yodh. Tenth Bullet," she said, and part of her shadow shone with an X before another shadow oozed out from it and was sucked into the barrel of the pistol.

And then, for some reason, she touched the photo and the CD to the side of her head and turned the pistol on them. It looked almost as if she were trying to defend against the bullet with the picture and the CD.

When Shido cocked his head to one side at the curious behavior, Kurumi pulled the trigger without hesitation. Hurtling out of the barrel, "Yodh" pierced the photo and the CD, and plunged into her head.

"K-Kurumi?!" Shido shouted, but then quickly realized something was amiss. Neither the picture nor the CD that the bullet had supposedly gone through were even scratched, much less Kurumi's head.

"Hee-hee-hee! I am quite all right," she reassured him. "The power of Yodh is recollection. This bullet brings me the memories contained in the target it passes through."

"The…memories?"

"Yes." She nodded, the corners of her lips turning up as she looked at the photo and the CD. "I see. So this is how everything developed. It's only fragments, but I've uncovered the reason why I felt something off about her."

"Y-you got something?!" he cried.

"Yes. It seems that Miku—"

The windows rattled, and he heard a loud sound from immediately outside.

"A-an alarm?!" His eyes flew open in surprise, but he soon realized that this was not the normal shrill spacequake warning he'd heard so many times in his life.

It was music.

The majestic sounds of an enormous pipe organ and a song woven together by a beautiful voice that took its listeners prisoner echoed throughout the city.

The moment he heard it, a familiar dizziness overcame Shido. He pressed hard on his temples to hold on to his mind.

"This is...Miku!"

Yes. This was the supreme performance by the Spirit Miku Izayoi and her Angel Gabriel.

But when he peeked out the window, he saw no sign of the enormous Angel. Most likely, it had plugged into the public speaker system that played warnings and other messages during times of emergency. That or she had one of those propaganda trucks driving around, blaring its speakers. He had already seen that Miku's performance had the power to affect people via machinery. So he knew the residents in this area would also become her ardent fans and move to capture him.

"...!"

Shido gasped and looked at Kurumi. But it seemed that, like Shido, Kurumi did not have her mind stolen when listening to Miku perform.

Still, the situation was growing progressively worse. Perhaps frustrated that she still hadn't found Shido, Miku was actively expanding her region of control.

"Oh my, oh dear. She does do things in quite a flashy way, hm?" Kurumi put a finger to her chin, seeming amused, but also annoyed. "Well, I suppose that's that then. Shall we walk and talk? At most, I will assist and only that. I shall prepare the venue one way or another. But the one who pulls the trigger must be you, Shido."

"Huh?" His eyes were as round as saucers, but he soon caught on to what she was getting at and clenched his hands into fists. "I need your help, Kurumi. We're going to talk to that spoiled brat."

"With pleasure," she responded, and lifted the hem of her skirt in a curtsy once more.

"_____!!"

Tengu Square's central stage was on fire.

An enormous pipe organ—Gabriel—rose up in the center of the stage, gleaming with a faint light, and Miku sang in front of it, running her fingers across the shining keyboard, clad in her Astral Dress. For the spectators, now transformed into Miku's crazed fans, this was a sight akin to a visit from God. People here and there passed out from the sheer overwhelming emotion of it all.

The men were chased out of the venue, so that the spectators who clamored in Miku's field of vision to take on the job of guarding her were all girls. They brandished the same purple light sticks and greeted each and every one of Miku's movements with shrieks and screams.

Her performance now was playing in real time over speakers all across the city. Anyone who heard her song would become Miku's newest soldier and set out to look for that despicable boy.

"...Unh!"

A memory of the loathsome incident a few hours earlier flitted through her mind, and she gasped unconsciously.

Her song ended at just that moment, and the venue erupted in applause that threatened to rip it apart.

Despite the fact that normally this would be a moment when Miku basked in that delicious sense of accomplishment and satisfaction, her mood now was sour because the face of that boy had just marred her thoughts. An indignant look appeared on her face, and she brought her mouth toward the mic she had yet to touch until now.

"I'm tired, so I'm going to rest juuuust a little. Feel free to do as you pleaaaase until I begin again."

She heard disappointed cries but paid these no attention as she turned and went back to the wings of the stage.

"Haah..."

She was actually tired after playing her Angel for so long in order to expand her area of control. She let out a short sigh and pulled up her hair, damp with sweat.

"Th-that was wonderful...Miss Miku. Um, if you'd like...here..."

A timid voice called out to her. When she glanced over, she found a small girl in a maid's uniform standing there, holding out a towel to Miku.

This particular fan—Yoshino—had been totally charmed by Miku's performance that day.

Wavy hair, beautiful eyes like sapphires. The girl was like one of those dolls you just wanted to pick up and squeeze. There had been an extra maid café uniform, so Miku had told her to change into it. The costume suited her so well, it should have been illegal. Unable to resist, Miku wrapped her arms around the girl.

"Aaah, you are so cuuuuute! I can't stand it! It's too much!"

"E-eep! Miss Miku...?!"

"Whoa! Miku, baby, you are surprisingly. Bold!"

Yoshino looked panicked, her eyes shifting from side to side, and the rabbit puppet on her right hand—Yoshinon—cried out in a shrill voice.

At first, Miku had wondered why she had this puppet. But from the stories she had heard, it seemed that this was Yoshino's extremely close friend. Plus, Yoshino was so cute doing this ventriloquist act that Miku just let it go.

After she'd had her fill of skinship with Yoshino, Miku planted a kiss on her cheek and let her go. Yoshino's face bloomed a bright red.

"Thank you, Yoshino. You brought this just for meeee, hm?"

"Uh. Um. Y-yes!"

Dropping her head as if to hide her beet-red face, Yoshino held out the towel in her right hand.

Miku accepted it with a "thank you" and wiped the sweat from her forehead. Of course, half of it had technically been wiped away when she hugged Yoshino.

She looked down at Yoshino once more, and a satisfied smile rose up on her face.

This was no ordinary cute little girl. She was a Spirit who manipulated water and cold—Hermit. That was the code name for little Yoshino here.

A Spirit. Yes. Just like Miku, she had abilities beyond human comprehension.

"Hee-hee! I reeeeally am lucky. To think that there were Spirits in the venue here!"

Yes. It was a complete coincidence that Yoshino heard Miku's song. Miku never dreamed that she would be able to make a Spirit hers so soon. And not just that...

"Keh-keh, you must be enervated, Lady Miku. Best that you rest and take your leisure."

"Encouragement. Come this way, Miss Miku."

Miku turned her head to find two girls waiting there, dressed in the same maid uniforms.

They looked so much alike that she almost wondered for a moment if one of them wasn't an image in a mirror. But when she looked very closely, she could pick out the individual differences of each twin.

The one with the theatrical manner of speech and behavior, determined look on her face, and bewitchingly slender body was Kaguya, while the one with the dazed expression, unusual tone, and exquisite proportions that might have even rivaled Miku's own was Yuzuru. Both were creatures known as Spirits, just like Miku and Yoshino.

Naturally, the twins currently adored Miku. Now, perhaps to thank her for her hard work, they had set up a chair and a drink for her in the greenroom.

"Hee-hee! Thaaaank you."

Miku smiled warmly and, following the twins' urging, sat down on the chair. As soon as she did, Kaguya began to gently massage her shoulders, while Yuzuru knelt down beside Miku and held out a glass.

Miku turned just her face in that direction and took a drink through a thoughtfully placed straw. The sweet and tart taste of fruit filled her mouth.

"Mm. That's so goood."

"Bliss. I am so deeply honored."

"H-halt! Why would you speak only to Yuzuru? Do you mean to say that my technique does not bring satisfaction?!" Kaguya cried out as she massaged Miku's shoulders. She was so adorable like this that Miku's face broke into a cheery smile.

"I'm sorry. Of course that's not what I'm saaaying. Your massage feels really great. It's heavenly."

"Keh. Keh-keh… Is that so? Acceptable then," Kaguya mumbled as she put her anger to bed. This was also very cute, and Miku's grin grew even wider.

Perhaps thinking that the Yamai sisters had taken Miku from her, Yoshino looked around frantically and then picked up a large hand fan nearby and began fanning Miku slowly.

"Thank you so much, Yoshino. That feels wonderful."

"Uh. Um… It's. O-okay…!" Yoshino said, looking bashful but also delighted.

"Aah…" Miku let out a sigh of ecstasy.

What a paradise.

Girls eagerly awaiting her song in front of a stage that was hers alone. And peerless beauties looking after her every need with such devotion.

It was simply too marvelous; Miku almost wondered if it was a dream. And in fact, she had pinched her cheek a couple times earlier. Naturally, it hurt every time.

But…

"Ngh." Miku scowled at the vexing memory that flitted through her head once more.

Shiori Itsuka. It brought back that name and the face that went with it.

"I'll never forgive you…Shiori…"

The hatred that swirled in her heart carried into her voice as she half

groaned, half murmured this. The sheer threat of it made Yoshino and the Yamai sisters gasp.

Miku had met her—Shiori, a member of the Raizen High School festival committee—a few weeks before the Tenou Festival.

She said she was on the volleyball team, and indeed she was a tall girl with strong arms. And she had a particular way of speaking that was quite brusque for a girl. Yes, Miku remembered only too well that this was the sort of girl she didn't come across too often.

In fact, if she were to be honest, she had liked the girl enormously. To the point where it wouldn't have been an exaggeration to say she was obsessed with her.

However...

What came along to quench this thirst of Miku's was a most evil betrayal.

"Hrngh..." Remembering that vile scene vividly now, she was overcome by an unbearable urge to vomit, and she pressed a hand to her mouth.

"M-Miss Miku!"

"Are you unwell, Lady Miku?!"

"Shiver. Someone get a bag."

The three Spirits cried out in a panic. Miku checked their movement with "I'm all riiight" and gritted her teeth tightly.

That abnormal sensation she'd felt when she touched Shiori's lower half. And then the terrible thing she had seen between her legs.

Yes. Shiori Itsuka was the type of creature that Miku loathed most of all in this world—she was a man.

"I'll get you. You'll pay! How dare you toy with my heart!" Miku hugged her shoulders as if to stop them from shaking and scratched at her upper arms.

All the things she'd done when she thought Shiori was a girl flashed before her eyes. With each image, goose bumps rose up on the skin all over her body.

There was one last thing she needed to do before she made this town her ideal home. She could never find rest until that man, Shiori

Itsuka—aka Shido Itsuka—was brought before her and she made him regret the fact that he had ever been born into this world.

"That boy... We stiiiiiill haven't found him?" Miku asked, her voice filled with wrath, which made Yoshino jump.

"N-no... Um. We haven't had any...word yet."

"Is that soooo... Have them continue—"

Just when Miku was about to give instructions, the door of the greenroom opened with a *bang*, and three girls in the same maid uniforms as Yoshino and the Spirits came running in.

"Excuse us, Miss Miku!"

"It's an emergency, Miss Miku!"

"It's real bad, Miss Miku!"

They shouted in order of height.

The Raizen students who were supposed to play in the band with Shido. Miku was pretty sure their names were Ai, Mai, and Mii, from right to left.

"What's the maaatter? Why are you in such a panic?" she asked.

The three girls looked at one another before continuing.

"I-it's serious! They found Itsuka!"

"*What* did you say?" Miku narrowed her eyes at this report, and laughter began to spill out of her mouth. "Hee-hee... Hee-hee-hee-hee-hee-hee-hee-hee! Is that soooo? They finally fouuuund him?"

She stood up slowly.

"He was more tenacious than I expected. Hee-hee-hee! But he can't fight me. He can't run from my adorable army. Where exactly was he found? If it was a girl who found him, I will spoil her most lavishly. Please ask the girl in question to come here later. If it was a man... Well, I suppose I could give him a candy."

Ai-Mai-Mii looked at one another with troubled expressions.

"What's wrooong?" she asked, and then gasped. "Oh! Is the person who found him maybe nonbinary?"

"N-no, that's not the issue..."

"How can we put this... Too many people found him."

"Or, like, we don't know where he was hiding..."

Miku frowned dubiously. "What are you trying to say? You found the target, right?"

"Y-yes."

"That's right."

"One hundred percent!"

The three girls agreed simultaneously.

"Then there's no problem, iiiis there? Where was he?"

"Um. That's... Quite nearby."

"Or more like, he's right in front of Tengu Square."

"Wh-what should we do?"

"Huh?" Miku's eyes flew open wide.

Chapter 7
A Siege of Two

A few minutes earlier...

With Kurumi at his side, Shido returned to Tengu Square, the large convention center in the center of the city of Tengu. The stage for the Tenou Festival, held jointly by ten different schools, was ground zero of the rioting ripping through the city. And the stronghold of the Spirit Miku Izayoi.

"Of course her base would have this many bodies around it," Shido said in a quiet voice as he peered down at the ground from the roof of a nearby building. Although it was very unlikely that they would hear him from so far below, there was still no need to speak loudly.

Countless people swarmed in front of the entrance to Tengu Square, which was eerily lit up in the middle of the night.

Noticing the sound of a propeller approaching, he hid himself in a shadow.

A news helicopter with the name of a TV station emblazoned on the side flew by overhead. They had no doubt come to get footage of the unprecedented riot, but most likely, everyone from pilot to reporter had heard Miku's performance. The helicopter had been persistently circling the area around Tengu Square at a strangely low altitude, as if systematically searching for something in the area.

He had no idea exactly how far Miku's control reached, but at the very least, the parts of the city that he'd seen on their way to Tengu Square had been filled with residents wandering around, their minds captivated by Miku's performance. The whole thing looked very much like a scene from a disaster movie.

And they hadn't been almost discovered just once or twice. If Kurumi hadn't been with him, Shido would have been caught long ago and delivered up to Miku.

"We made it this far. So what's the plan now?" Sweat beaded on his forehead as Shido looked down on the throng of people clamoring below him. "With the front door looking like this, the other entrances are bound to be locked up tight. And even if we wanted to break in through the roof, there's that helicopter watching."

"What are you talking about, Shido? Why, it goes without saying," Kurumi replied with a blank look.

"You have a way in?" he asked.

"Yes, of course. I will ensure that you are delivered directly to Miku. Well, naturally, after that, the rest is up to your own little tricks, Shido."

He frowned. "Can you really do that?"

"Oh my! Don't you have faith in me? My heart breaks. I feel as if I might burst into tears at any moment," Kurumi said, and covered her face with her hands in an overly dramatic gesture. "Waaah."

"H-hey, whoa…"

"I shall not stop crying until you give me one of your eyeballs. Or let me lap up your warm blood. Or pat my head and say, 'There, there.'"

"…There, there." He didn't have much of a choice. He stroked Kurumi's hair that rested above the blood-red dress.

She giggled happily. "Now, shall we be on our way? The situation will only grow worse with the more time we waste."

"…"

Shido stared through narrowed eyes at the very person who had been messing around just a second earlier. But this would lead to nothing except more trouble, so he decided not to say anything.

"What exactly do we do, though? With so many people watching, I mean—"

"Kee-hee-hee! Hee-hee! It's simple." Kurumi smiled luridly and stood up. And scooped Shido up while she was at it.

"Huh?" he cried out, baffled.

"Noooow, it's time for us to go." She put a foot on the edge of the roof, Shido still in her arms.

And then without a moment's hesitation, she leaped forward.

"W-whaaaaaaaaa?!"

A ten-story building. A vertical drop of more than thirty meters. Without even the chance to brace himself, Shido forgot about the swarms of enemies in the area and screamed.

He felt a sense of weightlessness lifting him up, and then they were landing. The moment Kurumi's feet touched the ground, a concentrated shadow appeared there to absorb the impact of their fall.

"Oh my, oh dear, Shido. You were quite loud there." Kurumi giggled as she peered at his face.

"Wh-whatever. Just put me down!" he yelped.

"Hee-hee-hee! I wouldn't mind staying like this myself, though," she said, setting him down.

Instantly, several spotlights lit them up clear as day.

But that was only natural. He'd screamed so loudly in the middle of a group of enemies on high alert. He had basically *asked* them to look this way.

"Crap!" Shido took in the scene before him.

Person. Person. Person. And as a bonus: person.

The enemy numbered in the tens of thousands. It was such an absolute disparity in combat strength that *overwhelming* didn't begin to describe it.

On top of that, they were all staring at Shido with hateful eyes as if he had killed their parents or something. No matter how brave the person, it was enough to make anyone at least break out into a sweat.

"Well, that really is so like you to go shrieking and telling everyone where you are, hm?" Kurumi said casually.

"And who's fault is that?!" he yelled.

But now was not the time for that.

Perhaps all these people were just watching them. Or maybe they were waiting for orders from Miku. Either way, rather than charging at them, a group of men were steadily building up a perimeter. They gradually formed a semicircle around Shido and Kurumi, who stood with the wall of a building at their backs, while brawny men and police officers with guns stepped forward to stand at the front of the human barrier.

"You must be feeling quite confident to go out of your way to return to my castle, hmmm, Shiori—No, Shido Itsuka!"

A voice rang out in Tengu Square. Although it was through speakers, there was no mistake. It was Miku Izayoi. She had clearly been informed of his presence.

"Miku!" Shido responded automatically. But naturally, his voice couldn't reach her inside Tengu Square.

Miku continued in the same ice-cold tone.

"I have noooo idea what you're up to, but now that it's come to this, I can't let you run anymore. You understand, right? All right, everyone, please capture him. You may hurt him if it's only a liiiiittle bit, but please handle him as carefully as you can, okay? Otherwise, there'll be less for me to do."

The announcement cut off with a *zzt*.

And then Shido heard the earthshaking roar of the Miku believers who filled his field of vision.

"Aaaaaaaaaaaaaaaaaaaaaaaah!!"

"G-gah!"

Freed of their fetters, the devotees bolted toward Shido and Kurumi in an avalanche of people. Shido had somehow managed to put on a brave face until that point, but now he flinched at the sheer force of the crowd.

"K-Kurumi! We're doomed! We gotta get out of here!"

However.

Kurumi didn't so much as turn her head as she continued to stand there calmly.

And this made sense only when he thought about it. Whatever else was going on, they were completely surrounded by an army of countless fanatics. There was already nowhere for them to run!

"Ngh!"

This was the end of the line. Shido pressed himself against the wall behind him as the hands of the man in the lead reached out for his neck.

But before those hands could touch him, the man dropped to the ground abruptly as if he'd been yanked down by a sudden burst of gravity.

"Huh?" Shido said, perplexed, and then put his hands to his knees. Because an extraordinary wave of fatigue washed over him as the man reaching for him collapsed.

"Wh-what..."

He mustered his strength and somehow managed to get himself to stand upright again.

When he looked around, he saw that the men surrounding them were all moaning in agony on the road. And that despite the bright illumination of the searchlights, a rich darkness lurked on the ground.

He knew this sensation. He had experienced this anomaly just once three months earlier when Kurumi had been attending his high school.

"Castle of Devouring Time?!" he gasped.

"Kee-hee! Hee-hee-hee! How astute of you. I see you remember it well, hm, Shido?" Kurumi's lips twisted up into a grin, and she turned her face toward Shido. The hands of the clock on the golden face in her left eye were spinning rapidly.

The Castle of Devouring Time. When Kurumi used her Angel's powers, she had to spend her own time, so to speak. But she was also able to replenish this time from outside herself. She put the people who stepped on her shadow into a kind of comatose state and extracted their time—their life spans.

"The trick really is to have a shadow spread out across a wide range," she told him. "Hoo-hoo-hoo! But I rarely have opportunities to receive time from such a large crowd. I will make sure to put it to good use."

"Kurumi, you—that's dangerous!"

"Oh my, oh dear." She arched an eyebrow at him. "Are you perhaps saying that it would have been better to be captured?"

"Ngh…" Shido gritted his teeth, pained, and stepped forward. "Just don't overdo it!"

"Yes, yes. I understand," she said. "The number of people being what it is, the hands are no doubt spinning quite dramatically. But the amount of time I'm receiving from any one individual is barely anything at all. Basically, they'll have plenty of time left as long as they make sure to take good care of themselves."

"…"

He had no choice but to believe her. Dragging heavy feet, Shido stepped out of the circle of fallen faithful.

"Wh-what? They…!"

In the Tengu Square security office, Miku cried out at the unbelievable scene unfolding before her eyes as she stared at the monitors lining the wall.

The screens were currently showing feeds from cameras set up on the roof. Miku had wanted to enjoy the spectacle of that loathsome boy being captured from this special seat, waited on by her adorable Spirits.

But just when her believers closed in on Shido under her orders, they all collapsed on the spot. And then, with no one left to block their path, Shido and a girl in a dress simply strolled away.

"That girl… Does this mean that she's also a Spirit?" Narrowing her eyes, Miku stared at the girl on the monitor.

Given what she'd just witnessed, that was the only assumption Miku could make. This boy Shido must have anticipated this development and held another Spirit in reserve. What a wily trick! Miku clenched her fists in vexation.

"Not to mention she seems in full possession of her mind when it should have been stolen by my performance. Hmph, this is annoooying."

The fact that the girl had made it this far meant that she had to have heard Miku singing, but she showed no signs of obeying the pop star. Miku had made Yoshino and the Yamai sisters her slaves, so it wasn't like her performance didn't work on this girl because she was a Spirit. Did she perhaps have the same ability as Shido?

As Miku's thoughts raced, Shido and the mysterious girl approached Tengu Square. They would soon be at Miku's doorstep.

To seal Miku's Spirit power.

"Ngh! As if I'd allow thaaat to happen." Miku squeezed the words from her throat, her clenched fists trembling.

Yes. There was absolutely no way she would let them steal her Spirit power from her.

After all, if I lose this power, this voice...

"It would be...just like back *then* all over again!" She shook her head briskly from side to side and leaped up from her chair.

Kaguya had been massaging Miku's shoulders, and now her eyes flew open in surprise.

"L-Lady Miku? Is something the matter?"

"I'm going back to the stage right now!" she cried. "Follow me! We're restarting the performance!"

"Hngh..."

It turned out that walking over a layer of unconscious people was a surprising drain on the human psyche. Battling the nausea that came over him from time to time, Shido chased after Kurumi, taking small bouncing steps like dance moves.

Although it was hard to say this was an easy path to walk, even if he were trying to be generous, there wasn't a single person actively obstructing them. It wasn't long before Shido and Kurumi reached the entrance to the central stage.

"Now, Shido."

"Right!" He nodded and shoved the door open.

"...!"

The atmosphere hanging over the central stage was also bizarre. The audience seating was filled with girls, but they were all bent over, heads hanging, possibly due to the effects of Kurumi's shadow.

And on the stage at the far end of the space, he saw her.

A girl clad in a shimmering Astral Dress stood calmly with a massive Angel in the shape of a pipe organ behind her.

Miku Izayoi. A Spirit who manipulated voice and sound—and the current queen of this venue.

He also spotted Yoshino and the Yamai sisters next to her, manifesting limited versions of their own Astral Dresses over their maid uniforms, with each of their own Angels at the ready.

"Miku!" Shido shouted.

Miku let out a great sigh. "Whaaaat is this voice? Could you please not sully my ears and those of myyyy Spirits with something that sounds so disgusting? You truly are an unpleasant person, hm? You've gone beyond having no value to being actively harmful. You're so repulsive that if you were turned to dust and returned to the earth, you would cast an eternal curse upon the land, ensuring no new life could ever grow there. Could you pleeeeease just keep your mouth shut, you walking cloud of pestilence?"

"...Ngh!" Showered in abuse in that slow drawl, he automatically furrowed his brow.

But he couldn't flinch at something like this. He called out to her once more.

"Miku! Listen to me! I have to go and rescue Tohka—the girl who was abducted before! So—"

"I said...please shut your mooooouth!" Miku shrieked, and threw out her hands.

A shining keyboard materialized in the empty space, following the trajectory of those hands.

"Gabriel! March!"

All her fingers pounded on the keyboard, and a stirring song filled the venue, the sort of tune that made a person stand up and move.

Instantly, the limp girls in the audience jumped to their feet like marionettes being pulled around by their strings.

"Th-this is..." He looked over at Kurumi.

But the clock of her left eye was still spinning counterclockwise. Meaning she hadn't released her Castle of Devouring Time.

Kurumi's eyes grew wide. "Oh my, oh dear. This is quite the surprise.

To think that a mere human could move while stepping on my shadow!"

"Hee-hee-hee! How do you like that? Isn't it amazing? The power of my Gabriel doesn't only make people adore me, you knooooow?" Miku smiled triumphantly, and her performance grew increasingly intense. "Now then, no more playing nice. No more orders to caaatch him. My adorable little girls! Please kill that boy!"

The thousands of girls in the audience all whirled to stare at Shido.

"Ngh!" He froze, grimacing.

But before the girls could attack him, Kurumi's lips curled up into a crescent moon and she laughed out loud.

"Kee-hee-hee! No, no, don't act as though you are victorious over such a trifling as this."

Her shadow painted the entire venue black.

"You can give these girls all the extra strength you want, but they still won't have a chance again *me*."

"Wh...?!" came Miku's perplexed cry from the stage. The reason was obvious.

From every area of Tengu Square's central stage, an area supposedly under the complete control of Miku's sound, countless Kurumis popped into existence and held down the hands, feet, and bodies of Miku's girl army.

"—?!"

Miku wasn't the only one stunned; for a moment, Shido was also at a loss for words before this unusual sight. It wasn't the first time he'd seen Kurumi's avatars show up. But the last time had been on the school roof, so there hadn't been this many of them crawling up out of the shadow all at once.

However.

Shido turned to Kurumi with a gasp. "Kurumi!"

"I understand. I won't kill them." She shook her head in exasperation, guessing what was on his mind before he could get the words out.

"Wh-what *is* this?! How on earth...!"

In response to Miku's screeching, the Kurumis growing out of the venue floor, walls, and seats giggled in unison. The bizarre sound echoed from all directions. The entire spectacle was disordered and absurd, a painting done by a mad artist.

But as to the question of whether or not Kurumi had now completely subdued Miku's troops, the answer was absolutely not.

"Raphael. El Re'em!"

"Concord. El Na'ash."

He had no sooner heard these voices from the air above than he was assaulted by an intense roaring wind.

"Hngaah!"

Shido was helplessly knocked through the air by the overwhelming blast and slammed into a wall.

But strangely, the impact didn't hurt at all. And why would it? A Kurumi avatar with just her torso poking out from the wall had gently stopped the flying Shido.

"Th-thanks, Kurumi... I *can* call you that, right?"

"Hee-hee-hee! Please don't stand on ceremony. I must keep you in perfect shape until I'm ready to *eat* you."

"...R-right." He had some complicated feelings here, but now wasn't the time for sorting them out. Planting his feet on the floor, he looked up at the two girls who leaped out from above the stage.

"Kaguya! Yuzuru!"

The twin Spirits, with Astral Dresses like bondage gear materialized over maid uniforms and a single wing on each of their backs, looked down on Shido, with enormous lance and pendulum at the ready. Kurumi might have been powerful, but even she couldn't casually restrain a Spirit who had materialized her Angel.

"Learning nothing from the past, you return then?! Keh! Your methods are mysterious! We show no mercy to any and all who would harm Lady Miku, whosoever he might be! Depart with haste if you do not wish to be embraced by purgatory!"

"Caution. This is your final warning. Disappear at once. If you attempt to strike her, Shido, we will be forced to remove you once and for all."

Kaguya and Yuzuru stared at him with cutting gazes from where they were floating in midair. They weren't fooling around. Their eyes were filled with a hostility so palpable, it almost took physical form and stabbed him.

"W-we won't let you…lay a finger. On Miss Miku!"

Similarly, Yoshino, plastered to the back of her large rabbit-shaped Angel Zadkiel onstage, had erected a barrier of cold air to defend Miku from the herd of Kurumis.

Seeing this, Miku's stiff face began to relax once again.

"Hee. Hee-hee! That's riiiight. I have three precious, adorable Spirits standing by me now! There's no way I can lose!"

The Kurumis laughed in unison again.

"Kee-hee-hee! Hee-hee!"   "Hee-hee-hee-hee-hee!"

"Aaah! Aaah!"   "True, true."

"Up against Spirits."   "With no Angel."   "Might be a bit."

"Of a disadvantage for us, hmm?"

Their voices echoed from all around, like wind whistling through a dense forest. This was disturbing even to Yoshino and the Yamai sisters. They grimaced uncomfortably.

"Now then, it's time!" Kurumi raised a leisurely hand and sang out the name of her Angel. "Come forth, Zaaaaaafkiel. Let us chastise these insolent and disrespectful Spirits!"

Instantly, a golden clock rose up from the ground, as if to block the entrance to the stage. Its massive face was perhaps twice as tall as Kurumi herself, and an ancient rifle and pistol were set upon it in place of clock hands.

"Her…Angel…," Shido murmured, staring up at the clock, dumbfounded.

Zafkiel. An Angel with the unparalleled power to control time.

The corner of Kurumi's mouth slid up, and she threw her arms out. The two guns popped off the clock face and dropped into her waiting hands.

And then Kurumi said quietly, "Now, Shido. Are your preparations complete?"

"Huh? Preparations?"

"I will ensure that you and Miku have a moment alone. Please do try to convince her somehow. It would be wonderful if you can find a way to reform her. If that proves impossible, then please do make her promise to at least not interfere with Tohka's rescue."

Kurumi winked as she kissed the pistol.

"Zafkiel. Aleph. First Bullet."

A shadow oozed out from the *I* on the clock face and was sucked into the barrel of the pistol. At the same time, new Kurumis holding guns popped out of various parts of the venue and began to fire shadow bullets at the Yamai sisters hanging in the air.

"Gah! How vexing! Yuzuru!"

"Response. Kaguya, give me your hand."

When the twin Spirits joined hands, they started to spin with that bond as the axis.

A fierce wind kicked up with the twins at the center of the vortex, easily knocking away the Kurumis' inky black bullets.

"Keh-kah-kah-kah! Did you believe such trifles would be effective on us, the children of the hurricane!"

"Rejection. Such an attack is nothing more than a peashooter in the face of our wind."

The Yamai sisters called out in loud voices. The Kurumis shot shadow bullet after shadow bullet, but all were caught up in the swirling wall of wind surrounding Kaguya and Yuzuru.

However.

The real Kurumi standing in front of Zafkiel twisted her lips up slightly at this sight. And then she turned the gun loaded with Aleph on the Kurumi who had caught Shido.

"Well then, I shall leave this to you, Me."

"Yes, I accept this responsibility, Me."

After this brief exchange, a black bullet pierced the Kurumi who held Shido.

But Shido knew that this was not a bullet that killed its target. The power of Aleph was...

"Whoa!"

Shido gasped at the sudden shock that assaulted his body.

For a second, he thought he'd been attacked by the Yamai sisters, but that wasn't right. With him still in her arms, the Kurumi avatar had slipped out beneath the sisters and was racing toward Miku on the stage.

"Wha—!"

"Shiver. Just now—"

He heard the baffled voices of Kaguya and Yuzuru above. Although this Kurumi carrying Shido in her arms had had her time sped up by Aleph, the sisters had apparently still noticed her. They clearly possessed an incredible dynamic vision.

But stuck repelling the bullets that came at them from all directions, the Yamai sisters were a second delayed in responding to the fast-forward Kurumi. By the time they began to glide through the air after them, Shido and Kurumi had already reached the stage.

"…!"

"Ah! Ah ah!"

Onstage, Yoshino and Zadkiel panicked at their sudden appearance and threw up a wall of ice to protect Miku from this new high-speed threat.

But several Kurumis immediately flew at Zadkiel like missiles.

"Kee-hee-hee-hee-hee-hee-hee!"

"A-ah!"

"Whoa! What is with *all of you?!"*

Yoshino yanked her hands back, and Zadkiel turned away. The moisture in the air around them condensed into icicles. These icy daggers shot out in all directions to counter the charging Kurumis.

When Yoshino was forced to deal with this onslaught of clones, her formation of the barrier on the stage slowed. An instant before the ice wall was complete, Kurumi closed in on Miku, Shido in her arms, so fast she was nothing more than a blur.

"Eee!"

"Bleh!" Kurumi playfully stuck out her tongue at Miku.

The other Spirit apparently did not care for this. The fear on her face was instantly replaced by anger. She threw her head back and took a deep breath.

"Kurumi! Watch out!" Shido shouted. He had seen Miku do this before. That pressure of the sound she produced the last time he saw her do this had enough force to send Tohka flying. However sped up Kurumi's time might have been, she wouldn't be able to dodge it, given that it was a sound.

But then something unexpected happened.

"Aah!"

An inky shadow spread out at Miku's feet, and a Kurumi leaped out and slapped a hand over Miku's mouth.

"M-mmph?!" Miku darted her eyes about in surprise and kicked and flailed to try and break free.

But more Kurumis crawled out of the shadow to wrap themselves around Miku's limbs. And then they slowly dragged her down into the shadow.

"Hngh! Mmmmmmmnph?!" Although she struggled frantically, Miku wasn't physically strong enough to fight off this many Kurumis. Gradually, she was swallowed up by the darkness at her feet.

"K-Kurumi! What are you doing?! This isn't what we—" Shido cut himself off and gasped.

His own body, still held by Kurumi, had started to sink into the shadow as well.

"Wha—?! Kurumi!"

His eyes flew open in surprise, and he squirmed to try and get away, but Kurumi's hands held him firmly. His field of vision steadily descended, as if he were on an elevator.

"Ngh... Ah!"

"Kee-hee-hee! Hee-hee-hee-hee-hee-hee!"

Listening to Kurumi's peals of laughter, Shido watched as his world was colored black.

"...Huh?" He blinked rapidly in the darkness.

He had been swallowed up by Kurumi's shadow, but his mind and his body still seemed to be intact at the very least.

Frowning, he looked around. There was only a vast inky shadow in all directions. He couldn't see anything else.

"Is this… I can't actually be in Kurumi's shadow, can I?"

"Aah! Honestly! What is going oooon?! Where am I?"

He heard a familiar voice from behind, so he turned around and looked in that direction.

"Miku?!"

"…Mm!" Miku had also spotted Shido. For a moment, her eyes were round in surprise, but the shock on her face was quickly replaced by disgust, and she threw her head back as if to scream.

But that action was stopped before it could begin. The shadow filling the area tangled itself around her.

"Eee?!" Miku flinched.

A muffled voice came at them from nowhere and everywhere. *"Kee-hee-hee! You mustn't get up to any mischief, Miku."*

The quiet laughter of several people echoed in the darkness.

"Now then, I've kept my first promise. The rest is in your hands, Shido. However, we haven't much time. Please do hurry."

"Uh. Right…" Shido's cheeks twitched helplessly.

Kurumi had indeed promised to get him alone with Miku, but he couldn't help feeling that her methods were a bit forceful. Or that she could have at least explained all this to him beforehand.

But this likely would have been the only way to come face-to-face with Miku when she was guarded by her immense army and the Spirits Yoshino and the Yamai sisters. Shido considered the situation and turned back to Miku.

"Miku."

"…Hmph." Miku whirled her head away.

She didn't show any signs of attacking him—perhaps because she more or less understood the situation she was in—but she was clearly not interested in hearing him out regardless. She scowled unhappily and crossed her arms, as if to say they had nothing to discuss.

Shido stepped over to stand in front of her and bowed deeply. "First, let me apologize for lying to you. I'm really sorry!"

She glanced at him and then sniffed haughtily.

"You're the worst. Absolutely the woooorst. After hiding the fact that you're a boy to do this and that to me, you have the audacity to show me that disgusting *thing*!" she said, her hands trembling.

"...No, *you* were the one who did those things. And you insisted on looking—"

"What are you trying to say?!" she snapped.

"O-oh..." He quickly shook his head. He didn't need to go saying anything extra and getting her all bent out of shape. "I was wrong to lie to you! But...please don't drag all those people into this! Release everyone under your control right away, and Yoshino, and Kaguya and Yuzuru—"

"Shut. Uuuuuup!" Miku tore at her hair and shouted, sounding very worked up. "Please be quiet please do not taaaalk! Y-you embarrassed me so much, and now you're making demands?! I do not want to hear a word from you!"

"M-Miku—"

"Please do not act so familiar with me!" Miku yanked her face away.

"H-hey."

"..."

"Miku."

"..."

She was completely unapproachable. This was a problem he needed to solve before he could even begin to get to the heart of why he needed to talk to her.

"Well, this sucks..."

However, he had anticipated this situation. Right from the outset, he hadn't believed he'd be able to win her over in this short time, not when he already had the worst likability with her.

That was why Kurumi hadn't told him to persuade her to their cause.

He just needed her not to interfere when they tried to rescue Tohka.

If he could make her promise that, then Shido would have fulfilled his bare-minimum role here.

"Miku. You can stay like that. Just listen to me."

"..."

Miku gave no reply. But Shido continued speaking anyway.

"Tohka— When we were onstage, there was a girl playing the tambourine, right? That's her. I'm sure you noticed, but Tohka's a Spirit, too, just like Yoshino and the Yamai sisters. And you must have seen it, Miku. Tohka was abducted by a DEM Wizard."

"...!"

Perhaps this triggered something in her or maybe she was simply reacting to the word *Spirit*, but at any rate, the completely unresponsive Miku had just twitched the slightest bit.

"I...I'm going to rescue her," Shido said.

"...Huh?" Miku turned just her head and spoke at last. Although her face was adorned with the most displeased expression yet. "Rescue? Why would you go and do that?"

"Why? Because Tohka's important to me, obviously," he replied.

Her eyes widened in surprise, and then she snorted in contemptuous laughter. "'Important,' he says. Oh, I seeee. Is that how it is? But there's just one thing I don't understand. She is indeed a beautiful girl, and honestly, I have to say you're seriously out of your depth."

"...Huh?" Shido cocked his head to one side, unable to grasp what Miku was saying.

"I mean, you're simply lamenting the loss of someone who will take care of your sexual urges. Buuuut it all comes to naught if you die, you know? They do say where there's life, there's a way."

"Wh-what are you talking about?" he asked, dazed, forgetting to object to the rude nature of her statement.

"I *meeean*, when a man says *important*, it always really means *that*, doesn't it?"

"...You have some serious prejudices, huh?" Shido said, frowning.

"Ha!" Miku jerked her chin up, scornfully. "So what then? Are you saying that this Tohka girl is moooore important than your own life?"

"Of course." He didn't even have to think about that one.

"..."

Perhaps Miku hadn't expected this. She twisted up her face in a way he'd never seen before.

Regardless, Shido continued speaking.

"No matter what happens, no matter what I have to do, I'm going to rescue Tohka. And when I do, I'm going to come back here. Next time, I can come alone, without Kurumi. So Miku, would you please wait quietly until then without doing any more damage?"

"...Uh?" Miku sounded displeased, her hatred still clear on her face. "Are you telling me to truuuust you? More importantly, eeeeven if you're not lying, you won't be able to reach Tohka, will you? You'll just get killed along the way by some Wizard. So sorry, so sad, rest in peace."

"That's—" Shido tried to argue as Miku clasped her hands together in front of her chest, like she was making fun of him, but then he stopped himself. Or rather he was forced to stop.

To be honest, he couldn't entirely rule that possibility out.

It was true that he currently had the aid of Kurumi, who possessed the strength of literally more than a hundred people. But that didn't mean DEM would be a walk in the park. Even if he was able to get Tohka out safely, he had absolutely no guarantee that he personally would come out unscathed.

If he at least had one more person on his side. If he could gain the assistance of a Spirit, then it would be a different story...

"Ah!" Shido yelped.

He didn't know how Miku interpreted this cry, but she lifted her chin up, seemingly triumphant.

"Do you understand at laaast? That's right. There's no way you can make a promise like that. So then—"

"Right," he interrupted her. "A promise."

Her cheeks twitched in doubt and displeasure. "That's what I've been saying this whooooole time."

"Not that. I'm talking about a promise that's already been made. The promise that *you* have to keep."

"Me?" Miku said, annoyed, as she cocked her head to one side, and then gasped.

"Looks like you've remembered," he said quietly, staring into her eyes. "Come on, you promised. You said if we won on the first day of the Tenou Festival, you'd let me seal your Spirit power."

This had to have been a sore spot that Miku didn't want poked. Bringing it up again risked another temper tantrum from Miku and could trigger an explosion of violence.

Except that, right now, Miku and Shido were inside Kurumi's shadow, where absolutely no act of violence was permitted. There was no better place to carry out negotiations as equals. Miku also had to have understood this.

Gritting her teeth with irritation, she turned sharp eyes on him. "Th-that promise isn't valid! You hid the fact that you're a boy—"

"And I apologized for that. But what does the fact that I'm a boy have to do with your promise?"

"Unh… I-I was the one who won the performance division!"

"Yup. You totally did," he said curtly. "But the *winner* is the one who took the grand prize. Weird. Aren't you actually the liar here?"

"That's absurd! A-and I mean, sealing my Spirit powers… I will never, neeeeeeever let you do that!" Miku shouted. There was no longer any reasoned argument here. She was simply pitching a fit.

However, backing Miku into a corner wasn't his goal here. If he pushed any harder, she would only become more entrenched in her position. He held out a hand as a peace offering.

"Yeah? Well then, let's make a deal. We can change the promise to seal your Spirit power to something else."

"Something else?" She raised an eyebrow.

"Uh-huh. If you do just one thing for me, we'll call it square," he said, holding up his index finger.

"What are you talking abouuut?" Miku scowled, not hiding a bit of her hatred. "That won't change anyth—"

"Help me rescue Tohka."

"Huh?" Her eyes grew wide as saucers. All the refusal and guardedness on her face slipped away. "Th-that's your condition?"

"Yeah, it is." He nodded. "I hate to admit it, but you're right. I don't know if I'll be able to actually rescue Tohka, even with Kurumi's help. But if you were there, too, we might be able to make it happen!"

"Buuut... Your goal is to seal my Spirit powers, right? So why would you do this?"

"I told you. Because that's how important Tohka is to me," Shido replied simply.

"...!"

Miku scowled again. Almost as though to say she didn't believe him.

"Hmph! I refuuuse! First of all, why should I do that anyway?!"

"M-Miku..."

"I've had enough! I do not want to hear anything you have to say! It's all lies! You have ulterior motives! A selfish creature like a human being would never care that much about anyone!"

"Miku, you're going on about that again?!" Shido clenched his hands and frowned in disgust. Even after he'd learned her secret from Kurumi, he still didn't understand this about her. "Why do you look down on human beings like this?! I mean, you're—"

A ray of light shone into the world of inky darkness, interrupting him.

"...?!"

When he looked up, he saw something like a crack in the black space and stiffened unconsciously.

For a second, he thought maybe Miku's shouts had caused the shadow to break. But if that really were the case, it seemed highly unlikely he would simply be standing there unscathed, not when he was so close to her. And Miku herself was also looking around like she had no idea what had happened.

Just as a question mark popped up above his head, he heard Kurumi's voice coming from somewhere.

"I apologize for the rude interruption. Unfortunately, our time here is up."

"Huh? Wh-whoa?!"

"Eee?!"

He felt a sudden buoyancy like he was being yanked upward, the opposite of the sensation from when he'd been pulled into the shadow.

His head shook intensely, colors other than black charged into his field of vision, and a moment later, Shido and Miku were tossed onto the stage at Tengu Square.

"Unh. Eh…"

Maybe because he'd just been yanked out of the dark shadow, his eyes stung a little. But they quickly adjusted to the light, and he was able to take in the situation onstage.

Several Kurumis had banded together to guard Shido and were facing off against Yoshino on Zadkiel, and Kaguya and Yuzuru with Raphael readied. It wasn't hard to catch the open hostility in their gazes.

"M-Miss Miku…!"

"Lady Miku! Are you well?!"

"Relief. You're safe."

Yoshino and the sisters cried out when they saw Miku come out of the shadow with Shido.

Kurumi knelt close to him. "Can you stand, Shido?"

"Kurumi… What on earth was that…"

"I told you, didn't I? Time limit," Kurumi said and looked around. "In order to leave people inside my shadow, I must leave it open. If the shadow is injured, the space will quickly collapse. I bought you as much time as I could, but things don't go very smoothly when your opponent is a group of Spirits."

He turned his head to follow her gaze and saw innumerable Kurumi corpses fallen around them. It had apparently been quite the intense battle.

"The supply of my time is not inexhaustible. And so we will be retreating now."

"Wait a second! I just need a little more—" His collar was abruptly yanked up, and Shido stopped speaking. "*Cough!* Wh-what are you…!"

A massive icicle plunged into the spot where he had just been, and he couldn't actually continue his protestations.

When he looked back, the warm and kind Yoshino was glaring at him with eyes filled with malice.

"I-I can't let…Miss Miku's enemy live…!"

"Y-Yoshino…"

"Do you understand the situation now?" Kurumi said, sounding somewhat exasperated as she turned the pistol in her hand upward. "Zafkiel. Aleph."

She shot herself with the fast-forward bullet, grabbed Shido with her free hand, and leaped up.

"Ah?!" He unconsciously cried out at the intense g-force that pressed down on his body.

But Kurumi paid this no attention as she set her feet down on a light fixture and danced up into the night sky through the hole in the roof.

Miku wasn't about to let them get away, however. Pressing a hand to her forehead as if trying to hold back the drunken sensation of being pulled up out of the shadow, she shouted, "Pl-please don't let him escape!"

"Understood!"

"Roger. We have heard you."

The Yamai sisters flew outside in pursuit of Kurumi.

Kurumi might have been using her high-speed bullet, but her opponents were wind Spirits. If they got into a protracted battle, they might very well overtake her.

"Oh dear, oh my. This is a bit of a pickle, hm?" Kurumi said in a voice that had none of the nervous tension of her words, and she raised the pistol in her hand once again. "Zafkiel. Bet. Second Bullet."

A shadow shot out from the stage and was sucked into the barrel of the gun. Kurumi turned this toward the Yamai sisters and pulled the trigger.

"Hmph! Ignorant girl! Such a trifle has no effect on us!"

"Restraint. Please wait, Kaguya. That is—"

As she raised a voice in warning, Kaguya and Yuzuru froze where they were.

No. To be more precise, they hadn't quite stopped completely.

It was extremely slow, but they were still moving forward. They were not frozen in place; their movements had just been made incredibly slow.

"What was that…?" Shido asked with a gasp.

"Kee-hee-hee! Bet. This bullet delays the progression of time for whatever it hits," Kurumi replied. She was speaking deliberately slowly so that Shido could hear her, but even so, she sounded a little like she was on fast forward. "Zayin's actually much more certain, but the mileage on that one is terrible. Especially since right now I must keep a reserve of time. Still, this will do just fine if we're simply trying to run away."

Just as she said, the distance between them and the Yamai sisters steadily increased. The wind Spirits might have been proud of their impressive speed, but they couldn't keep up with the accelerated Kurumi after being hit with a bullet of slowness.

With Shido in her arms, Kurumi danced up into the darkness of the night and disappeared into the city.

The effect of Aleph wearing off at last, their speed dropped abruptly. Kurumi slipped from building to building, hiding, and finally set Shido down.

"Well, since we're here. Shido, come this way a little."

"Huh? O-okay." His head felt like he'd just gotten off a super-speed roller coaster, and he allowed Kurumi to take his hand and lead him into an alley.

In the next instant, there was a loud roar right before a mass of wind shot past in the sky above. He didn't have to wonder what it was. The Yamai sisters. They were looking for Shido.

"Oh my, oh dear. Bet doesn't steal away consciousness, and even with that tremendous difference in our speeds, they were able to see us, hm? Honestly, where do they get their incredible vision from?"

"…Ngh." He knew the sisters couldn't hear Kurumi's voice at this distance, but he still swallowed hard with a nervous look on his face as he stared up at the sky above.

Two small typhoons circled the area for a while, scattering the clouds until they flew off in a different direction. They showed no signs of giving up on the hunt.

He waited until he could no longer hear the sound of wind and then heaved a sigh of relief at last.

"So, Shido, how did things go with Miku?" Kurumi asked as she dropped the gun in her hand into her shadow.

Shido bit his lip before answering her. "Mm. We managed to have more of a conversation than I expected. But I didn't get a clear answer from her. I actually made her mad at the end to boot. Sorry, Kurumi. This was my mistake. You worked so hard to get me this chance, and I flubbed it."

Kurumi's eyes opened wide in surprise. "Oh my, oh my, oh my."

"Wh-what?"

"Oh no. It's that I simply never dreamed that you would offer me words of gratitude. Hee-hee-hee! This makes me so happy. Would you be so kind as to pat my head?"

"Qu-quit making fun." Shido lost his composure and sighed.

Kurumi laughed, amused. "Well, I suppose it will be fine. From what I heard, she won't go out of her way to court danger and interfere with us. At any rate, you were able to make her feel on guard against me."

"Ooh. I guess, yeah," he agreed, sweat popping up on his cheeks. It was true that having personally experienced the threat Kurumi posed, it would have been rather strange if Miku wasn't wary of her. At the very least, she probably wouldn't make a casual grab for him as long as he was with Kurumi.

"Honestly, what a disappointment." Kurumi lowered her eyelids and snuggled up against Shido as she licked her lips.

"Wh-where'd that come from?!"

"I left all the persuading to you, and I didn't want to overstep and inject myself into the conversation... But there was one part of your conversation with Miku that I didn't particularly care for."

"A part you didn't care for?"

"Yes," she half murmured. It was an entirely unremarkable word, but because she had uttered it so very close to his ear, a shudder ran through Shido's body. "You tried to have Miku come over to our side, yes? Say, Shido? Were you meaning to say that you're dissatisfied with my assistance?"

"Th-that's not what I...!" He couldn't bring himself to finish the sentence. It was true that he was anxious about having nothing more than Kurumi's help when they were going up against an enemy with unfathomable resources.

He heard a quiet laugh in his ear and then felt his earlobe being licked.

"Eee?!" He shuddered reflexively.

"Hee-hee!" Kurumi pulled away gently, her lips curling upward. "That was merely a joke. The enemy's combat strength is indeed an unknown variable. Your judgment that we should attempt to increase our own power at that time is commendable, and I have no intention of speaking ill of it... But still..."

She traced his lips with her index finger. The gesture was so obscene that Shido was at a loss for what to do and froze in place.

"Silly Shido." She shook her head from side to side. "You really are a terrible liar."

"Sh-shut up..."

"Oh dear, oh my. I am, in fact, complimenting you in a way, though?" She turned lightly as if dancing and finally pulled her finger away from him.

Freed at last, he let out a sigh of relief.

As if in line with that, the shadow spreading out at her feet wriggled and grew larger, and suddenly another Kurumi was crawling up out of it.

"Whoa!" Although he knew a certain amount about Kurumi's abilities, he was still surprised at the abrupt appearance of that same face.

But the new Kurumi showed no sign of shock or displeasure at Shido's reaction. Instead, she looked at him almost fondly before bringing her face close to the original Kurumi's and whispering something in her ear.

"Mmhmm. I see," Kurumi said, pressing a finger to her chin. "Very nice work. You may go."

The Kurumi who had whispered at her whirled around toward Shido, picked up the hem of her skirt, and curtsied elegantly before disappearing into the shadow.

"Wh-what was that?" he asked.

"Oh. That was a me I had acting independently looking for information."

"Information? So then—" When it came to information, he could think of only one thing at the moment. His eyes flew open, and he stared at Kurumi.

"Yes." She dipped her head forward in a leisurely gesture. "I have discerned where Tohka is."

"R-really? Where?! Is she okay?!" Shido asked, leaning so far forward, he was practically biting into her.

Kurumi looked shocked for an instant and then giggled. "You truly do adore her, hm, Shido? I'm quite jealous. I might just have to add another condition for my cooperation in her rescue."

"Condition?"

"Perhaps I could have you say 'I like Kurumi more than you' to Tohka's face."

"H-hey…"

"Hee-hee-hee! I'm only kidding." Kurumi stuck her tongue out at him playfully.

Whenever he talked with Kurumi, he got all twisted up. He cleared his throat to get himself back together and turned his eyes on her once more. "So then… Where'd they take Tohka?"

"Mm-hmm." Kurumi slowly lifted her face.

"Deus Ex Machina Industries Japan branch. Building One. It seems that that is where Tohka is confined."

"Now. Next question. Have you heard the word *Ratatoskr* before?" Ellen asked in a flat voice from where she sat next to Tohka inside a cold, austere room, flipping through the sheaf of documents on her lap.

"Hmph!" Tohka sniffed indignantly, lowered her eyes, and turned her face away. "Like I'm going to answer you!"

"I see. Very well, moving on. Do you know the reason why Shido

Itsuka is able to control an Angel?" Paying the apparent resistance no mind, Ellen continued with her questions. They had been going like this for a while.

It was the one being questioned who grew tired.

Tohka let out a sigh.

"Ellen, right? You were the photographer on our school trip."

"You remember me? I'm honored."

"Why exactly would a photographer do something like this?" Tohka asked. "You can't make a living on photography alone?"

Ellen frowned slightly. "No, being a photographer was merely a disguise. It's not actually my job."

"Mm? You're a photographer, but you're not a photographer?"

"No, what I mean is—," Ellen started, scratching her cheek awkwardly, when a voice came over the speaker-type device set in the upper part of the room.

"Please stop. It's dangerous! In the worst case—"

Ellen frowned dubiously. "Is something the matter?"

"O-oh! It's just he's saying he wants to go into the isolation room!"

"Come in here? Who exactly?" Ellen asked, and the voice over the speaker paused briefly before continuing.

"M-Mr. Westcott..."

"Ike?"

A man's voice came over the speaker. *"Aah, can you hear me, Ellen? Mind helping me out here? No one will do as I ask. I'm dismayed at how unpopular I am."*

"They're all concerned for your well-being. Please don't make trouble for them."

"Mmm. I guess that's one way to think about it. But this is a bit of a dilemma. In the end, which is superior, subordinates who do as I say or subordinates who worry for my safety?"

"At any rate, I belong to the latter group."

"Don't say that, my sweet Ellen," said a gentle voice over the speaker, and Ellen looked exasperated for the first time that day.

"It's fine," she said. "Please allow him inside."

"But...! Are you sure?" the original voice asked.

"Yes. Even if the Spirit does attempt anything, there won't be any issues as long as I'm here."

"*U-understood. Please do be careful!*"

A few seconds later, a crack appeared in the wall as it had earlier, and something like a door opened up.

A man stepped through it. He was tall and slender. His dark silver hair and the sharp eyes that looked like they had been cut into his face with a knife were his most prominent features. He couldn't have been any older than his mid-thirties, but he was cloaked in a dangerous aura that felt far removed from his age.

"...!"

The moment he entered the room, Tohka was struck by an overwhelming feeling of nausea. It wasn't that he had a Territory deployed like Ellen did. But still, as soon as she caught sight of him, she felt like the temperature around her dropped sharply.

"Wh-what are you—?!" She shuddered and glared at him.

The corners of his mouth curled up as though he could read her thoughts. "It is a pleasure to see you, Princess. Or wait. I suppose it's Tohka Yatogami."

He slowly walked toward her. With each step, the discomfort Tohka felt grew stronger.

"I am Isaac Westcott of DEM Industries. Pleased to make your acquaintance." The man—Westcott—spoke with familiarity as if he were chatting with a friend.

But Tohka poured every bit of hostility she felt into her eyes and glared at him.

"I suppose she hates me then?"

"If you wanted her to like you, you should have considered your methods more carefully," Ellen said.

Westcott shrugged. "You're quite right."

Tohka managed to somehow push back the urge to vomit that was rising up from her stomach and turned hard eyes on Westcott. "So you're the ringleader! What—! What exactly is your objective?!"

Westcott turned his gaze back toward Tohka and opened his mouth quietly. "Objective? Well, that itself is an extremely simple story.

I want your Spirit power." One side of his mouth slid upward as he continued.

"So that I can overturn the order of this world."

"What...?" Tohka frowned. She had no idea what he was talking about. "Maybe you got the wrong idea somewhere? I don't have that kind of power!"

"Mm-hmm, that's true. At least not the *you* you are right now."

"The me...right now?" Tohka said doubtfully.

Westcott spread his hands in a theatrical gesture. "The you in this world is far too stable. That's why we must first have you go to sleep. Yes. Just like when you drifted on the ocean of that parallel world. Actually, it might be more accurate to say I need you to *wake up* in the parallel world."

"What...are you..."

"You." Westcott's eyes narrowed abruptly. "What exactly can I do so that you will despair?"

"What...?" Tohka stared at him blankly.

"Filled with hate for the world, loathing its inhabitants, and even the most powerful Angel will not be able to fill the cracks that open up in the heart. You will have to cling to some other power. What can we do to put you in such a state? A look at the AST records shows that you were in a nearly ideal state once. So what happened?"

Westcott turned toward Ellen.

"What do you think, Ellen? Applying physical pain might indeed be the quickest way to go about it. We'll try electrical current first. And let's reduce the level of oxygen in the room and see how she reacts. We could also tweak the air pressure. If none of that works, we'll pull out her fingernails one by one. And then shave away her fingers bit by bit... Oh! I know. Let's file her teeth down, too. Nerve pain is so hard to bear."

"Wha..." Tohka paled. A chill ran up her spine.

The many tortures that Westcott listed were horrifying. But more than that, Tohka felt a fathomless terror as she regarded the man who so casually rattled off cruelties as if he were making suggestions for supper that night.

Whether he caught on to these thoughts of Tohka's or not, Westcott continued in a bright tone.

"The body of a Spirit is far tougher than that of a human being. Maybe we could try poisoning her, too. Ahh, in that case, pumping drugs into her is also on the table. And, oh yes, you have quite a strong sense of virtue, hm? If we thoroughly trample your dignity as a woman, how much would you suffer? You have been living in this world for some time now—do you have friends? A lover? How would you feel if someone you love was killed in front of you?"

"...!" Tohka unconsciously stiffened. She remembered when Shido had almost been killed by Origami.

Westcott nodded leisurely. "Ellen."

"Yes. The person she is likely closest to is that Shido Itsuka. Her reaction is different only when his name is mentioned."

"I see. Excellent. Then how about we wait for him before we continue?"

"Understood."

Westcott nodded, turned, and was about to leave the room.

"Hold it! What are you going to do to Shido?!" Tohka couldn't help but shout at his back, and she tried to rise from the chair. The manacles binding her hands creaked slightly.

But an invisible pressure immediately pushed her back down into the seat.

"Ah! Gah!"

"Please be still." Ellen's voice was cold.

"Shido..." Calling his name in a hoarse voice, Tohka's consciousness sank into darkness.

Chapter 8
City Sunk in Flame and Shadow

"Aaah! Come on! This is so, so, so, so, soooo annoying! A mere human making a fool of meeeeeee!" Miku pounded the table in frustration at a restaurant in a luxury hotel not too far from Tengu Square.

Anxious about Miku, whose agitation hadn't diminished since the attack mounted by Shido Itsuka and the mysterious Spirit at Tengu Square, Ai-Mai-Mii had proposed that maybe she could have supper and unwind a little.

Naturally, everyone in the hotel from employees to guests were under Miku's control. She had the restaurant all to herself, and the table where she sat alone was crammed with extravagant dishes.

But no matter how much delicious food she ate or how many cute girls she admired, Miku's frustration didn't lessen in the slightest.

"M-Miss Miku, please try to stay calm."

"*Yeah. If you're angry all the time, you'll ruin your adorable face, you know?*"

Yoshino and Yoshinon made their comments from where they stood behind Miku and wiped away the sauce that her hand had knocked flying when she banged on the table.

"This is quite correct. You were selected by the heavens above, an absolute, sublime existence. There is no need for your heart to be in turmoil over the words of Shido."

"Affirmation. It would be auspicious to forget all about such a person. If you concern yourself with him, there will be no end to it."

Kaguya and Yuzuru each placed a hand on Miku's shoulder gently.

"Y-yes. You're right. I don't need to bother myself with the poiiiintless ramblings of such a worthless person," Miku said, as if to convince herself, bobbing her head up and down.

But in that instant.

Because Tohka's important to me.

Shido's voice echoed once more in the back of her mind, and Miku slammed her fist down on the table again. Plates bounced up, and drinks spilled from glasses onto the tablecloth.

"Important? What does he mean, important? It's simply ridiculouuus. He's drunk on his own feelings. Aah, honestly, just remembering it makes me soooo annoyed! A human being—and an inferior creature of a boy at that—could never believe that anything is more important than his own life! It's simply impossible!"

Miku threw the knife and fork in her hands onto the table and ran her hands through her hair.

Exactly. The flowery words human beings uttered were all cheap and shallow, nothing but surface-level fawning. They couldn't be trusted. People were just trivial, worthless beings. It was obvious. They had to be.

"Otherwise, I—"

"Miss Miku…?"

She snapped back to the present with a gasp at the sound of Yoshino's worried voice. She waved the unasked question off lightly before turning her eyes on the girls in maid uniforms lined up behind her.

"Girls? You go to the same school as Shido and Tohka, riiiight?" she asked, and Ai, Mai, Mii, and the Yamai sisters all nodded.

Yoshino alone opened her mouth timidly after exchanging a glance with Yoshinon on her left hand. "Uh. Um… I. Don't. I'm sorry."

"But you doooo know both of them, right?"

"Y-yes…! Of course."

"Then there's no problem." Miku turned her chair around, crossed her legs, and gazed at each of her maids in turn. "I want you to answer me honestly. What is this Shido person to Tohka? Do you really think that Tohka is important to him?"

"..."

At Miku's question, the line of girls looked at one another as if deep in thought for a few seconds. And then they all nodded in agreement before turning their eyes back on Miku.

"Nah, he's a super-shallow guy. He'll tell you he likes you or you're important to him like it's the air he breathes. He's always sniffing around us, too."

"Yeah, totally. It's like his brain is directly connected to his junk. Or actually, maybe that's where his brain is to begin with. It's that bad."

"Thinking on it further, he's got no character. The whole thing with Tohka's gotta be just talk. I'm telling you, it's nothing for you to worry about, Miss Miku."

"..."

Listening to Ai, Mai, and Mii, who were very clearly looking anywhere but at her, Miku let out a sigh and her expression softened.

"I told you that I wanted you to be hooooonest, didn't I? I'm pleased that you would be so considerate of me, but I haaaate girls who lie," she said, pulling her hair back, and Ai-Mai-Mii jumped quite noticeably.

And then they sighed in resignation.

"The relationship between Itsuka and Tohka...right? Hmm, to be honest, I don't really know. It doesn't seem like they're dating or anything, but they're not just friends, either."

"Right, yes. Oh, but it's true that they're always together. Tohka seems genuinely happy when she's with Itsuka, and watching them kinda just makes you wanna smile."

"Yeah, uh-huh. Itsuka does love Tohka in his own way. He's always watching out for her no matter what's going on. They're super close."

"Hmm. They are?" Narrowing her eyes, she turned toward the Spirits. "So say there was a situation where he had to risk his own life to save Tohka... What do you thiiiink Shido would do?"

"Uh. Um," Yoshino mumbled reluctantly. "Miss Miku, it's okay...to be honest. Right?"

"Yes. All you have to do is tell me about the Shido that you knooow."

"Okay...then. I think Shido would do it... I think he wouldn't hesitate to save Tohka. Even... Even if it meant he'd die."

"..."

Miku bit her lip.

Perhaps noticing this, Yoshino let out a small "Eep!"

"And do you two share the same opinion?" she asked as she turned her gaze toward the Yamai sisters.

The girls put fingers to chins thoughtfully and then replied.

"Kah-kah. Well, Shido might indeed do such a thing. You'd do well to wager on him. That fool would step into the land of death with no regard for his own well-being. He would do the same for myself and Yuzuru as well."

"Affirmation. To put it bluntly, there must be something wrong with him. For Tohka's sake, he would definitely give up whatever was necessary to accomplish his goal."

"..."

Miku's scowl grew deeper.

Of course.

His words echoed in her head once again.

Because that's how important Tohka is to me.

"Ngh!" Miku clenched her fists in irritation and jumped up from her chair. She stuck her hands in her hair and yanked them back and forth. And sighed. "Today has been exhaaausting. I want a shower. Please set up a room for meee."

"Y-yes!"

"As you!"

"Wish!"

Ai-Mai-Mii snapped to attention and threw open the door to the restaurant as if leading the way for Miku.

Miku walked toward it on heavy feet. As she was about to step through the doorway, she turned her head to look back.

"Please have the citizens look for Shido. I don't care if I'm asleep when they find him. Pleeeease inform me right away."

"Huh? You mean..." Ai-Mai-Mii's eyes grew round in surprise. Miku's narrowed.

"It's obviously for revenge! All right? Please dooo as I say!" she shouted, and stomped down the hallway.

It had been about two hours since the hands of the clock passed their zenith and started downward again.

Beneath the moon and scattered stars, Shido and Kurumi had their eyes fixed on the cluster of buildings that rose up ahead of them.

"So this is where Tohka is?" he murmured as he looked around.

They were on a corner of the business district in the city of Kagami-yama to the east of Tengu. The hour being what it was, there were few people on the road where the skyscrapers with a smattering of lit-up windows stood, radiating a strangely intimidating presence.

He could also see a remarkably large building ahead from the road where they were standing.

"Have you noticed it?" Kurumi said from his side, perhaps seeing where his gaze was directed. "The section starting here is DEM facilities. Every last building you can see are affiliate companies, offices, laboratories, and so on."

"All of these..." He looked out at the buildings again and gulped. But he couldn't falter now. Somewhere in there, Tohka was being held captive. "So then, which one's Building One?"

"Mm-hmm. That would be the large building in the center of this cluster. Unfortunately, I haven't been able to discern where exactly inside she is."

"Okay..."

"But that won't matter at all if we don't first make it to the building. We should avoid being discovered if possible. Now then." Kurumi whirled around to put the wall to her back and turned her face toward Shido. "We are about to sneak into DEM. But before we do, it might be a good idea to have a little tête-à-tête."

"Meaning?"

"Yes, well. The plan itself is very simple. First, you and I will move toward DEM Japan Building One. Is this acceptable thus far?"

"Uh-huh."

"But this is DEM's base in Japan. It's hard to imagine that they would leave it defenseless."

"I guess that's true," Shido agreed unhappily.

They were up against the Realizer manufacturer DEM. It might have been the middle of the night, but he still had his doubts that they would carry out a large-scale battle with witnesses around in the center of town. Nonetheless, they couldn't be too careful.

"That is why once we arrive at our destination, I will call *us* up and launch an attack on the other facilities."

"I get it." He nodded thoughtfully. "So we take advantage of the chaos and slip inside the building. But if you start such an obvious attack, won't it actually put them more on guard? I mean, DEM has to be keeping an eye out to make sure that Tohka doesn't get taken back from them."

"It's true that Tohka is the most prized sample in the entire facility at the moment," Kurumi agreed. "If the premises come under attack, they will likely first tighten up their guard around her."

"Right. So then—"

"So don't you think that breaking into the building where this precious Tohka is confined is next to impossible? In which case, the clever choice is to draw their eyes to the other buildings. However important Tohka might be, that doesn't mean that they can completely ignore the fact that their other facilities are being attacked."

"Mm-hmm." Shido nodded, a hand pressed to his chin. It was simple, but effective. And there was no doubt that this strategy would have been impossible in practical terms if it wasn't being implemented by Kurumi, who could manifest an army of thousands at the drop of a hat. "Got it. Let's do it."

"I'm delighted to have your consent. Now then, shall we be on our way?"

"Yeah!" He clenched his hands and sharpened his gaze before stepping out toward the cluster of DEM buildings together with Kurumi.

The moment they passed down the road and set foot on DEM premises, they both frowned simultaneously and exchanged glances.

A familiar sensation. It was faint, but he felt something like an invisible brush stroking the surface of his body.

"Hey, just now—," Shido started to say and then stopped.

Actually, to be more precise, he was drowned out by a louder sound.

Vwnnnnnnnnnnnnnnnnnnnnnnnnnnnnnmmmmm.

An earsplitting noise began to echo around them.

For a moment, Shido thought it was maybe an alarm to detect intruders. But that wasn't it. He'd heard this sound before.

"The spacequake alarm?!" he cried out, scowling.

Yes. It was the area-wide alarm that sounded when a spacequake was detected—the unique catastrophe that coincided with the appearance of a Spirit.

"Does that mean a Spirit's gonna show? Here?!"

The timing was unbelievable. Shido glanced around, a tense look on his face. Stunned office workers doing overtime and convenience store clerks began to evacuate. The entrances to the underground shelters opened, and the city shifted into spacequake mode.

But Kurumi narrowed her eyes slightly and half whispered, "No, it doesn't appear that that is the case here. I don't sense any of the tremors that accompany a spacequake. At the very least, I don't believe that a Spirit is going to manifest here from the parallel world."

"Then what on earth is this alarm?" he asked.

"This is at best a supposition," she said. "But most likely, DEM is ringing this alarm. You appeared to have also felt it, Shido. A sensation as though we were touching the Territory of a Wizard?"

"Huh? B-but this is the spacequake alarm...right?"

He cocked his head to one side, not understanding DEM's intent. It didn't seem like this alarm was ringing only inside the facilities. It was the general alarm to urge residents in the area to evacuate. He knew DEM had inroads with the government, so maybe they were able to turn on the spacequake alarm. But that wasn't the sort of thing you set off just because you'd discovered an intruder.

"It is, isn't it? As for possibilities we might consider, for instance—"

Kurumi pressed a finger to her chin to show that she was thinking about those possibilities before she grabbed on to Shido's collar, kicked at the ground, and leaped back to the left.

"Hngh?! Wh-what are you—" Shido tried to voice his objections to Kurumi suddenly yanking him up by the neck, but then stopped.

The reason was simple. A beam of light had pierced the spot where they had been standing, causing an explosion and leaving a large hole in the ground.

"Wh-wh-wh…"

"—they might intend to carry out extreme violence to reduce the number of witnesses." Kurumi threw her head back to look up.

Shido followed her gaze. And then broke out into a cold sweat.

In the sky, against the background of the moon and the buildings, were several silver dolls wearing CR units.

Heads with what looked to be full face helmets. Unpleasantly developed arms, legs that bent backward with no regard for the limitations of human joints. He had seen their strange forms before.

"Those are Bandersnatches!" Shido cried, and the Bandersnatches turned as one to point the barrels of their laser cannons at Shido and Kurumi. They didn't hesitate to open fire.

"Whoa!"

"Tch!"

Kurumi tucked Shido against her side and leaped up.

The magical light released by the Bandersnatches ripped into the ground, producing a small explosion. The fleeing office workers stared at this in disbelief before hurrying into a shelter.

"Us!" Kurumi shouted after landing again with Shido in her arms, and instantly, a shadow spread out at her feet.

As soon as nearly a hundred Kurumis appeared, they leaped in perfect sync toward the Bandersnatches hanging in the sky.

"Kee-hee! Hee-hee-hee-hee-hee-hee-hee-hee-hee-hee-hee-hee-hee-hee-hee-hee-hee!"

It was a magnificent sight.

Kurumis jumped up onto the Bandersnatches dancing through the sky and began using their bare hands to tear off wings, guns, arms, legs, heads. If a Bandersnatch had the same awareness as a human being, this scene would no doubt have plunged them into abject terror.

Naturally, the Bandersnatches didn't just sit back and allow themselves to be destroyed. They fired laser cannons and micro missiles, causing bright red flowers to bloom on the heads and chests of the Kurumis, but the difference in numbers was simply too great.

A shrill buzzer like a shrieking death knell, red lights blinking on their heads, the Bandersnatches turned to lumps of metal and dropped to the ground.

"H-holy smokes…," Shido breathed.

"We don't have the luxury of admiring the sight. Reinforcements are coming," Kurumi said as she glared out over the premises, her guard still up.

Most likely, these Bandersnatches were some kind of patrol devices. More dolls in such number that the initial patrol didn't even begin to compare and Wizards appeared from the buildings up ahead. Some came out through the front door, of course, but the wall of the building also shifted and opened up to both sides, revealing a group of Wizards. Shido couldn't get an accurate count of how many, but there had to have been at least five hundred of them.

"Wha…?!" he cried out, stunned. He'd thought there would be some kind of defensive system, but he never dreamed it would be this army.

"Mm-hmm. All right then. Shido, we're going to alter our strategy a little."

"Huh?"

More and more Kurumis crawled out the pitch-black ground. They each pulled two guns out of the shadow and got into formation to counterattack the incoming Wizards.

"*We* will tackle the dolls and the Wizards," Kurumi told him. "We'll use that opening to slip through their defensive line."

"O-okay!" It wasn't like he had a choice now. Shido nodded firmly.

"Now then. I shall advance at top speed. Please cling to me quite tightly so that you are not thrown aside! Zafkiel. Aleph!!"

Kurumi pulled a pistol out of the shadow, pressed the barrel to her own temple, and fired.

At the same time, the vanguards of the DEM Wizards and the Kurumis crashed into one another. The Wizards exchanged laser cannon blasts and missiles with the shadow bullets of the Kurumis, causing massive explosions.

"—!"

In the arms of the sped-up Kurumi, Shido slipped onto the raging battlefield.

Intense g-forces pressed down on his entire body as multiple blasts ripped through the air too close for comfort. His ears rang, and for a moment, he thought he might pass out.

"Ngh!"

He bit down on the inside of his cheek hard enough to almost draw blood and forced himself to stay conscious. Before long, they were out of the battlefield—literally the epicenter of an explosion—and Kurumi slowed. The effect of Aleph had worn off. She was back to her usual speed.

"Are you all right, Shido?" she asked.

"Y-yeah… More or less," he said, and managed to stand on his own two feet again. His head felt a little unscrewed, but he couldn't bother with that now. He pursed his lips and refocused, clenching his hands into fists. "Okay. We don't have any time to waste. Let's go."

"Yes. Building One is—"

She started to point with her index finger and was suddenly colored black.

"Ah."

Quietly. Together with this truly quiet cry, the head of the Kurumi he had been talking with flew up into the air.

"Huh?" Shido gaped, unable to grasp what had happened because of the suddenness of it all.

A heartbeat later, warm blood jetted up from the spot where Kurumi's head used to be, dyeing Shido red, and only then did he finally realize what was going on.

"Unh. Aaaaah?!" he shrieked and fell over backward.

Kurumi's body crumpled to the ground like a broken rag doll.

"K-Kurumi! Kurumi!"

It was obvious that she was already dead, but Shido raced over to her anyway. The headless corpse twitched, creating a puddle of red liquid on the ground.

It was then that he noticed someone standing behind her. Out of the corner of his eye, he spotted feet wrapped in inorganic metal armor.

"Ah!"

There was no mistake. This was the CR unit of a Wizard. Most likely…a DEM Wizard.

He had to run. He knew that, and yet his feet wouldn't move. He gasped and turned his gaze upward.

The unit was blue and black, one he'd never seen before. The left hand was equipped with a weapon that looked like a massive maw, and the sharp form was reminiscent of a savage wolf somehow.

"Goodness gracious. I finally found you."

But hearing the high-pitched voice coming from this Wizard, Shido gasped, and his eyebrows jumped up. He looked up farther, toward the face.

Hair tied up in a ponytail, determined eyes. A beauty mark beneath the left eye. And a face that resembled his own somehow.

"Mana…?" His eyes grew wide.

Yes. It was the girl who said she was his actual blood sister—Mana Takamiya.

A few months earlier, after being seriously injured in the battle with Kurumi, she had been hospitalized and absolutely no visitors were allowed. It looked like she had made a full recovery without Shido's knowledge.

However. While he was surprised by the unexpected reunion, he nonetheless braced himself. Mana was originally a Wizard loaned out to the AST by DEM. The fact that she was there now meant one thing—she was going to eliminate the enemy that had infiltrated the DEM Industries facility. Shido.

But the moment she met his eyes, her face relaxed and she dropped to her knees to wrap her arms around him.

"Brother! I'm so glad that you're safe and sound!"

"U-uh?!" Surprised by the hard feel of the unit Mana was wearing, Shido darted his eyes about. But he quickly regained his composure and pushed on her shoulder to peel her off him. "M-Mana... It's you, right? You're all healed up?"

"Yes, I am! I'm going full speed, full health!" Mana bent an arm to show off her muscles, and Shido was more and more at sea at this cheerful voice that was so out of place in the battlefield around them.

"Uh. Um. Mana? You're a DEM Wizard, right? So then you came to take me—"

"No. We'll have to discuss the deets later, but I quit DEM."

"Huh? But this equipment..."

"Ohh. I stole this from *Fraxinus*. Ratatoskr's taking care of me now."

"Uh...What?!" His head spun at this string of new information. Why was Mana with Ratatoskr? Didn't the AST and thus DEM have totally opposite values from Ratatoskr? "But then why did you do that to Kurumi..."

"Oh! It looked like you were being attacked by Nightmare, and I couldn't just sit back and do nothing," Mana told him, and Shido raised an eyebrow.

Now that she mentioned it, although he was, in fact, working with Kurumi at the moment, she was actually Mana's mortal enemy and a human-eating Spirit. It was only natural that Mana would get the wrong idea seeing the two of them alone.

"Sh-she wasn't, though! Kurumi's helping me right now!"

"Helping you?" Mana narrowed her eyes suspiciously.

In the next instant, a black shadow spread out like a stain on the wall of the building, and Kurumi's face popped out with a twisted smile on her lips. At the same time, the corpse of Kurumi on the ground was swallowed up by the shadow.

"Kee-hee-hee! You did give me a rough welcome just like you always do, hm?"

"Kurumi!" he cried. "You're okay?!"

"Yes. You didn't honestly believe that something so trivial would

kill me, did you?" Kurumi laughed as she stroked her neck with a finger.

When exactly had she switched places with an avatar?

"That's too bad." Mana clicked her tongue exaggeratedly. "An extra second or two and I could have erased that hyper-creepy smile permanently."

"Haven't I told you before? You absolutely can't."

"Ha! How about we give that a test? All you have to do is hit me with those precious bullets of yours."

"Kee-hee! Hee-hee-hee-hee-hee! For someone who's still alive because of my personal whims and pure coincidence, you truly are delightfully naive. Or did you lose your memory from the sheer terror of it all?"

"Wow!" Mana said. "For the crazed murderer that you are, it's unusual that you're only coming at me with this lip service. So you don't even have the extra energy to get a challenge out to me?"

"Hee-hee-hee!" Kurumi giggled. "Am I to assume that you are fine with me dismembering you beyond any hope of recovery? Maybe I can have my fill of you starting with that busy tongue."

Glaring at each other with eyes full of hostility and murder, Mana and Kurumi exchanged dangerous words. Stuck exactly in the middle of this, Shido felt a cold sweat on his back.

"H-hang on, both of you…"

But Mana continued to look at Kurumi with eyes so fiery, they should have set her skin alight.

Kurumi sighed and shrugged. "Well, you have good timing if nothing else. I have another bit of business with DEM, so let us go our separate ways here. You'll be fine so long as Mana is with you, okay?"

"H-hey!" he protested. "Kurumi?"

"Please rest assured. The diversion *we* are using will continue. Well then, take care!" Kurumi lowered her eyes and dove into the shadow. A heartbeat later, the shadow vanished from the wall.

"Kurumi! Kurumi?!" he shouted, but got no reply. It seemed that she really had gone off somewhere. Shido scratched at his head, messing up his hair.

"Hmph. I don't know what kind of truce you negotiated with her, but it's better this way. I mean, cooperating with a monster like that, you don't know what kind of compensation she'll come asking for later."

"Mana, you..."

"Anyway. Excuse me a sec."

Looking like she couldn't have cared less about Kurumi, Mana stared hard at Shido's face before hurriedly patting his chest and then sighing with relief.

"Hey! Wh-what was that even?!" he cried.

Mana got a serious look on her face. "Oh, when I saw you on the video on *Fraxinus*, you were dressed in this strangely cute way. I thought maybe you had awakened to new tastes during the time I was away from you."

"I did not!" he shouted.

"Yes. I'm relieved. It seems that you didn't go so far as to rush into anything permanent." She paused. "What about downstairs? You didn't actually take it off, did you?"

"Of course not." He stared at her in disbelief. "What do you think I am?"

"Well then, let's call it fine. I am open-minded. I have the capacity within me to accept a bit of eccentricity if it's on the level of cross-dressing. I'll even go shopping with you one of these days."

"I'm telling you that's...!" Shido sighed heavily as Mana pressed on her ear and frowned. Loud voices were coming from her headset.

"Ohh... Yes, that's correct, that's right. Brother here." Mana pulled a small electronic device out of a pouch on her waist and offered it to him.

"Is this...an earpiece?" he asked.

"Yes. Take it. It's connected."

He accepted the earpiece and put it in his right ear. Soon after, he heard an awkward voice.

"Shido, can you hear me?"

"Kotori? You came back to your senses?!"

He knew who it was without asking. This was the voice of his own little sister and the commander of Ratatoskr.

Kotori had also heard Miku's performance over the speakers and become a fervent believer in Miku, just like Yoshino and the Yamai sisters.

"*Yes. Well. More or less,*" Kotori said, and then continued, sounding more reluctant. "*Sorry about that. It... That wasn't how I really felt.*"

"Huh? About what?"

"*The whole...you know. All that 'die' and whatever. I mean...I can't remember it, but there's video, and I guess...I said some stuff like that.*"

"Ahh." Shido nodded. Now that she mentioned it, he felt like Kotori had indeed said things like that while bewitched by Miku's performance. Apparently, this bothered her. He smiled automatically. "I know that much at least."

"*Mm...,*" she said, sounding embarrassed.

"Anyway, how'd you break Miku's control?" he asked, and heard Reine's voice in response.

"*...We had her cleaned out using Mana's Territory after knocking her unconscious. When everyone was under Miku's control, they messed around something awful with Fraxinus's transmission settings. It took a while to get them back to normal. Sorry we couldn't contact you until now. I'm just glad you're okay.*"

"No, I mean..."

"*...But don't worry. The earpiece Mana gave you now is set to automatically cut any sounds outside of a specified range. Miku's performance won't reach us here again.*"

"Gotcha," Shido said.

"*Now to get to the main issue.*" Kotori cleared her throat, as if to switch gears. "*Shido, what are you doing there? And with Kurumi, of all people.*"

"Oh, that's..."

Shido briefly explained what had happened while Kotori and her crew were under Miku's control: Ellen had abducted Tohka, Kurumi was helping him rescue her, and Tohka was being held captive in this facility.

Kotori was silent for a moment. And then...

"*No. Too risky. I can't approve this,*" she said in a solemn voice.

He furrowed his brow at this unexpected answer. "Wh-what are you talking about?! They took Tohka! And DEM is a dangerous organization, hellbent on killing Spirits, aren't they?! We have no idea what they're doing to her!"

"*I don't need you to tell me that. I know!*"

"So then why?!"

"*You're trying to say I shouldn't stop my brother from jumping right through the front door of this dangerous organization?! Wake up! You never include yourself when you're worrying about who might be in danger!*"

"Ngh!" He groaned. "S-so you're saying we should abandon Tohka?!"

"*I'm not saying that! But we have to prepare first!*"

"How can you be so heartless?! All the Kurumis are keeping the Wizards tied up right now! We'll never get another chance like this!"

"*That's—*"

"Please, Kotori!" he begged. "I... I *will* bring Tohka home! So please!"

"*...Argh! What do you think this is?!*"

He heard Kotori hit her armrest in frustration.

"*You're not gonna listen to me, are you?*"

"You get it then."

"*I haven't been your sister for over ten years for show, you know.*" Kotori sighed in what sounded like resignation and then continued. "*Most likely, communications inside the building will be blocked by a Territory. We won't be able to guide you from here. All we can do on* Fraxinus *is give you external support.*"

"That's plenty," he said gratefully. "Thanks, Kotori."

"*Honestly. The struggle never ends for those of us with an older brother who just won't listen, right, Mana?*"

Mana's shoulders shook with silent laughter. "Yes. Although any weakling who would run away with his tail between his legs wouldn't be a brother of mine."

Kotori sighed for the nth time. "*Very well. If you're going to do this,*"

I won't accept anything less than one hundred percent. Tohka rescued, Shido and Mana safe. Anything less is a failure."

"Right," Shido replied.

"Well then, shall we," Kotori continued, with a prepared speech.

"Yes. We shall," Shido replied.

"Begin our date?"

"Begin our date," he said, and turned his face toward Building 1.

Rewinding the clock a little. Two AM.

Origami groaned where she lay on the hospital bed, opening and closing her fists.

Although she still felt a dull pain in her head, she was now able to make her body move more or less how she wanted, maybe because of the medical Realizer treatment she'd had earlier. The doctor had told her she was on strict bed rest, but she felt like she might actually be able to go look for Shido now.

"..."

She turned her head silently to one side.

"Uwah, O-Origami... That's a crime, you know..." Mikie muttered slightly rude things in her sleep, leaning against Origami's bed. She was fast asleep. This was Origami's chance. She sat up without making a sound.

She had to confirm Shido's well-being as soon as possible. Jessica and the DEM Wizards who were after Shido and Tohka had been mopped up by Mana, but she was concerned about the riot that Ryouko mentioned. She hoped he was okay.

She slid off the bed and stuck her feet into a pair of slippers there, and then froze in place.

Having been brought to the hospital in her wiring suit, Origami had no change of clothes.

How to deal with this? As she racked her brain to find an answer to this question, Mikie turned slightly in her sleep.

"Origami... I told you no... You'll get sick if you eat that..."

Origami looked down at the girl. She was wearing a high school uniform.

"..."

There was a slight difference in their heights and physiques, but an ill-fitting uniform was still a much better choice than a hospital gown. Origami decided on her course of action as expediently as possible, laid Mikie down on the bed, untied the ribbon at her throat, and unbuttoned her blouse. She then pulled down the zipper on her skirt and very gently undressed the other girl, being careful not to wake her.

Vwnnnnnnnnnnnnnnnnnnnnnnnnnnnmmmmm.

A shrill alarm began to sound outside the window.

"...! A spacequake alarm?" Origami furrowed her brow minutely as her hands lifted up Mikie's skirt.

"Mm... Unnh... What's that noise?" Naturally, Mikie woke up. She yawned, rubbed her eyes, and stared at Origami vacantly. "Oh... Origami. Good morni—eeah?!"

In the middle of this greeting, she realized the state she was in and leaped up as if she were having a seizure. Her face turning bright red, she yanked the blanket up to cover her naked chest.

"O-O-O-Origami?! I would like to ask what on earth it is that you are doing?!"

"I was taking off your clothes," Origami told her plainly. There was no point in lying now.

"Whaaaaaat?!" Mikie's face was already tomato red, but it grew even riper. "Wh-what were you planning to do after taking my clothes off?!"

"After I took them off? I was going to take off mine, too, obviously."

"Ah! Aahyaaaaah?!" Mikie shrieked like an exotic beast and pressed her hands to her cheeks.

Did she hate the idea of someone else wearing her clothes that much? Maybe Origami had done something bad here. She bowed her head and returned the skirt in her hands to Mikie. For some reason, this made Mikie's shoulders jump up.

Then the skirt she had just returned began to vibrate. Apparently, Mikie was getting a call.

"Oh! Y-yes! Okay!" Mikie hurriedly fumbled around in her pocket and pulled out a communications device. "Yes, this is Okamine... Oh! Right... Uh-huh... Wait. Wh-what?!"

Her opened her eyes wide in surprise. She said a few more words and then hung up.

"What happened?" Origami demanded.

"R-right." Mikie paused to collect her thoughts. "Um. DEM's Japan branch was attacked by a Spirit and a...collaborator. AST members are to mobilize immediately and provide DEM support."

"Attacked? What's the code name of this Spirit?"

"N-Nightmare."

"...! Kurumi Tokisaki?" Origami narrowed her eyes sharply. That name belonged to a Spirit who had transferred into her own class. "Then who is this collaborator?"

"Th-that's..." Mikie averted her eyes, seemingly reluctant to tell Origami.

She grabbed her face in both hands and forced Mikie to meet her eyes. "Answer me."

"R-right," Mikie said. "It's...Sh-Shido Itsuka."

"Shi...do...?" Origami repeated, stunned.

"...!"

She whirled around toward the door of her hospital room.

"O-Origami!"

But she couldn't run for it. Mikie had grabbed her left hand.

"Y-you can't! Do you understand the condition you're in right now?!"

"Doesn't matter," Origami replied flatly. "I don't know what his reasons are, but if Shido is on the battlefield, then I have to help him."

"H-how exactly?!"

"There should be some equipment remaining in the AST hangar," she said, and Mikie shook her head vigorously.

"It's impossible! Your authentication ID has been frozen! You can't use the proper equipment!"

Origami frowned, stopped moving, and turned her eyes on Mikie. "What do you mean?"

"Just what I said!" Mikie cried. "You don't have permission to use a wiring suit right now, much less a CR unit!"

"..."

Origami gritted her teeth. That only made sense. She had taken equipment out without authorization more than once now and pushed her brain beyond the activation limit. There were plenty of reasons to freeze her out.

But even so, she couldn't simply lie back down.

"Then regular equipment is fine. I should be able to take a firearm of some kind."

"H-have you lost your mind?!" Mikie cried. "Stepping onto a battle-field with Wizards and Spirits and no Territory of your own, it's basically walking into your own death! Please think about this calmly!"

"Someone very important to me is on that battlefield. So...I have to go."

"Ngh!" Mikie pulled even harder on Origami's hand. "Is he...that important?"

"Yes."

"More important than your own life?"

"Yes," she said, not even pausing to consider the question. "He's the last foundation for my heart now that I've lost everything else. If he dies, I'm certain I will stop being me. So let go."

Mikie's eyes narrowed sharply. "What if I said that if you go, I'll bite my tongue and die here?"

Origami looked into Mikie's eyes. "You wouldn't do that."

"...! Please don't underestimate me. I mean, that's how much I care about—"

"You wouldn't because you know it would make me sad."

"...!" Mikie's eyes flew open, and she hung her head. She put a hand to her face like she was wiping away tears. "I hate this... I'm jealous of him. Of the fact that you would go so far for him."

Mikie sighed and lifted her face.

"I won't be able to stop you?"

"No."

"You're going, even if it means heading out there with nothing but the clothes on your back?"

"Yes," Origami said, and Mikie smiled sadly.

She quickly put her clothes back on and jumped down from the bed. "I understand. If you've made up your mind, then I can't stop you. But I can't simply let you go out to certain death... I don't know if this will help or not, but I have an idea. Please follow me."

"An idea?" Origami cocked her head to one side curiously.

The magical bullets and small missiles fired by the DEM Wizards and the Bandersnatches blew away the paved roads and entire buildings where the Kurumis were clustered. Each time they did, lurid screams and peals of laughter echoed through the area, and Kurumi silhouettes danced up into the air like old rags.

But the inky black bullets blended in with the blowback and shot up into the sky, piercing the units the Wizards wore and the heads of the Bandersnatches.

It was a preposterous and wild melee that seemed impossible for this world.

Hundreds of thousands of minuscule bullets poured down on them freely like rain, and an inexhaustible supply of Kurumis crawled out of the black shadows toward the Wizards dealing overwhelming damage. The embodiment of the most terrible nightmares. Both sides were killing each other without mercy or hesitation. If Shido had set foot in that place, he would have been sliced into such tiny pieces that it would have been difficult to find a whole person's worth of a body for his funeral.

"..."

That was an unpleasant thought. Flying at low altitude supported by Mana's Territory, Shido cursed his vivid imagination and poked his forehead.

"There, Shido."

He heard Kotori's voice over the earpiece and lifted his face. Mana also turned her gaze in the same direction.

He saw a building that was significantly taller than the others around it. It had to have been at least twenty stories tall. A sturdy-looking shutter had been pulled down over what appeared to be the main entrance, perhaps because of the chaos that had broken out all around the building.

"Please hang on a waiting second," Mana said, and touched her feet to the ground.

At the same time, Shido wrapped in her Territory also moved slowly downward, as if his body had remembered the existence of gravity.

Mana placed the palm of her hand against the shutter and clenched it, speaking quietly.

The three-centimeter-thick shutter twisted up, and a hole big enough for a person to fit through appeared.

"Okay, let's go," she said.

"Amazing as always," he replied with a wry smile and followed her through the hole. "But this place really is big. If only we knew what floor Tohka was on at least."

He heard a sleepy voice over his earpiece. Reine.

"...If they've got Tohka locked up, that means they'll have a Spirit isolation facility. You remember the isolation area on Fraxinus? Look for something like that."

"Right. Makes sense." Shido felt that curious buoyancy envelop him once again. There was no mistake. This was Mana's Territory. "Mana? Why are you—"

He didn't get to finish his question. His body was suddenly thrust up as if shoved by an invisible hand.

The front entrance of Building 1 twisted and distorted, and his field of vision was filled with a dazzling light, which was followed by a massive explosion.

"Wha...?!"

Knocked back by the blast, he tumbled along the ground. His head throbbed dully where it hit the ground.

But he couldn't be distracted by that now. Shido lifted his face with a gasp.

"Mana! Mana!!"

"Yes, yes. I'm fine." Mana leaped out of the thick smoke. As far as he could see, she was uninjured. She had apparently quelled the impact of the explosion with her Territory.

But instead of relief and reassurance, her face was colored with tension and a hint of anger.

"It can't actually be...," she said quietly.

A massive lump of metal appeared from the large hole in the laboratory, cutting through the dense smoke that filled the area.

Two weapons like enormous trees. A heavy form like a tank. And on the back, a girl tucked away in the middle of all this machinery.

Shido's eyes flew open. He had seen this equipment before. "That's... White Licorice?!"

The enormous weapon that Origami had worn to take down Kotori. The one difference being that while Origami's had been a snowy white, the machine before his eyes now was the color of blood.

"I'm impressed that you're aware of this. But you're a little off. That's DW-029R, Scarlet Licorice. It's a sister machine to White Licorice made for experimental purposes." Mana spat out the words and scowled in annoyance. "Changing up your look? This is quite the different impression from when I saw you this afternoon? Ruins your darling little face, Jessica."

The passenger in Scarlet Licorice was a redheaded woman in her late twenties. Her eyes were somehow reminiscent of a fox. But it was hard to get a good look at her face for the simple reason that her limbs, chest, forehead, and face were wrapped in bandages.

"Ha-ha-ha! Mana Mana. Mana Takamiyaaaaa? So? Soooo? What do you think of my Licorice?! I can't lose with this. Not to you. Not a little thing like you!" The woman—Jessica—cackled with laughter despite the fact that she was seriously wounded.

"You know her?" Shido asked.

"Former colleague. Ridiculous," Mana said, and took a step forward.

"Jessica! Get out of the Licorice unit right now! You understand, don't you?! That's not a thing you should be operating!"

"Ha-ha-ha-ha-ha-ha-ha! What're you talking about? I feel great. After all..." Jessica's gaze sharpened, and she turned a gun toward Mana. "I finally get to kill you."

"Ngh!"

Picking up on this signal, Mana closed in on Jessica without any advance warning and maneuvered the laser edge in her right hand to cut her former comrade.

But Jessica had apparently anticipated this. As she caught this blow with the high-output laser blade she wielded with her left hand, the weapon container on her back opened up, launching countless micro missiles.

Dozens of projectiles exploded at super-close quarters that would have normally been unthinkable. An incredible blast of wind pushed outward, and Shido's field of vision instantly filled with smoke.

"Wh-whoa!"

Naturally unable to maintain his balance in the face of this, he flew backward. A blue silhouette cut across his field of vision, and an enormous red shadow chased after it.

The two Wizards took the battle up into the air and started fighting again. Missiles and bullets scattered in all directions, swords clashed, and every few seconds, magic light flashed in the dark sky like stars.

"Ngh..."

He would just have to let Mana handle Jessica. Even if he tried to help, he would only get in Mana's way.

Once he understood that, he acted quickly. He immediately stood up and raced toward the building.

"*Shido! It's too dangerous! You can't go in there on your own! Wait for Mana!*" Kotori roared, trying to stop him.

But Shido didn't slacken his pace.

"They'll tighten up security if I wait for Mana! I have to go now! And isn't it more dangerous for me to be outside by myself?! There's stray bullets, and that Jessica Wizard could even try to take me hostage! I can't drag Mana down!"

"Th-that's...maybe true, but! Hey! Shido!"

Regardless, he stepped through the entrance to the building, which was utterly destroyed inside. Instantly, Kotori's voice was swallowed by static roaring in his earpiece, and he could no longer hear her.

There was no one in the large lobby, only rubble strewn everywhere, blocking his path forward. Lights with exposed wiring hung down from the ceiling, flickering eerily, sending out a shower of sparks every so often.

According to Reine, there was a facility in this building for keeping Spirits isolated. Shido took the stairs two at a time.

"Haah! Haah! Haah!"

Second floor. Third. Fourth. Fifth. His legs gradually grew tired, and he was breathing so hard, his lungs hurt, but he ignored his body and kept going.

Tohka. Somewhere up ahead was Tohka.

The girl who had gotten him out of harm's way and been captured in his place was being held all alone in the belly of an organization that was out to get the Spirits.

When he thought about it like that, he didn't have any time to waste whining about the limits of his own body!

"...!"

After he'd climbed who knew how many sets of stairs, Shido noticed a suspicious sound and furrowed his brow.

A man and a woman were up ahead in the hallway. And they weren't general employees or researchers. They were both wearing wiring suits of a design he'd never seen before. Perhaps because they were indoors, they were each holding only a small firearm that looked like a handgun and a small laser edge. But they were, without a doubt, Wizards.

"Intruder?!" one of them yelled.

"Hey! You!" cried the other. "Who are you?! Where'd you—"

"Ngh!" Shido gasped, and ran down the hall to try and escape them.

The Wizards quickly deployed their Territories and came after Shido with incredible speed. He heard the sound of gunfire, and bullets cloaked in magic light left alarming holes in the wall.

"Stop! Stop or we'll shoot!"

"You're already shooting!" Shido yelled, and dodged bullets that plunged into the ceiling, the wall, and the floor as he raced down the hall.

But the difference in speed was plain. A few seconds later, he was pushed up against the wall as if restrained by invisible hands, probably because he had entered their Territory.

"Ngah?!"

"What's the big idea, leading us around on a wild goose chase like that? This boy's the attacker?"

"No way. Still, it's not like we can just let him walk away."

The woman held up a hand as if to pin Shido down, and the man turned the barrel of his gun on Shido.

"Ngh..." He gritted his teeth and squirmed around, trying to break free.

"Stop struggling. I guess we'll have to knock you out." The man raised his hand and brought it toward Shido.

"...! Dammit! I don't have time to be standing around here!" Shido shouted, and slammed his clenched fists desperately against the wall.

Something. Someway.

He frantically racked his brain. If he was captured here, he would have no way of saving Tohka.

"Tohka!"

Her face, etched firmly in his memory, flitted through his head.

Tohka. The first Spirit whom Shido had seen, except for that incident five years ago.

She laughed with him when he was happy. She sat with him quietly when he was depressed. When he was lost, she gave him a push and shouted encouragement.

He had no idea how much courage her innocent smile gave him. When Kurumi and the Yamai sisters showed up, Tohka had been right there beside him when he lost sight of what the right thing for him to do was.

He might lose that smile of hers.

The moment he realized this, a sharp pain ran through the depths of his heart.

"Like I'd let that haaaaaappeeeeeeen!" The shout ripped from his throat. "Wha…!"

He heard the Wizards' baffled cry, and his field of vision was filled with a dazzling light. He felt the invisible power holding him down start to weaken.

A heartbeat later, he realized there was something new floating in the space between himself and the Wizards.

A sword. A single massive sword shining with golden light.

"Wha… This is…Sandalphon?"

Yes. Tohka's Angel. A blade with tremendous power, Sandalphon.

And right now, it was hanging before Shido's eyes.

"Wh-wh-wha…?!"

"A-an Angel?"

In contrast to the shock he heard in the Wizards' voices, Shido was surprisingly composed. Because, of course, he had made Sandalphon appear from thin air once before.

The question was why Sandalphon had appeared here now. But upon further thought, he more or less figured out the answer to that.

"Aah, right. Let's go rescue your master," Shido said to himself, and then reached to grab the hilt of the enormous sword.

The Wizards shuddered and fired bullets coated in magical energy.

But these things had no meaning before the Angel. Just as the bullets were about to touch the blade, they sizzled and melted into thin air.

"What?!" one of the Wizards cried, baffled.

Shido ignored them and brandished his new sword. Naturally, he knew almost nothing about fighting, and that went double for swordsmanship. In fact, if someone had handed him a gun and told him to go defeat his enemies, given that he would have had no idea how to fire it, he likely would have used it as a blunt weapon, causing it to explode and him to die in an accident of his own making.

But. For just this one blade. For one blade in the entire world, Shido had been schooled in its use by its most powerful user.

I told you. Sandalphon was summoned now because of your wish, Shido. So you're the only one who can make it come true.

*   *   *

The words Tohka had spoken when he held Sandalphon the first time came back to him vividly.

Calm your mind. And remember. What do you want to do? What are you wishing for right now? Put everything else out of your mind. Imagine that wish in your heart and swing the sword. The Angel will respond.

A single wish. He focused all his determination on his wish to rescue Tohka.

Sandalphon grew brighter in response to Shido's will, thrumming with power.

"Aaaaaah!"

With a battle cry ripping from his throat, he swung the magic blade. Rings of light rippled outward from the arc of the sword and sent the Wizards and their Territories flying, along with the entire wall behind them.

"Nngh!" one of the Wizards grunted as he was propelled outside the building.

But one enemy remained standing before him. The Wizard rushed toward Shido as she drew her laser edge from her waist and swung it at Shido.

"Hngh!"

He just barely managed to raise Sandalphon in time to defend himself.

The Wizard clearly had him beat in terms of speed. She dropped down low and thrust a large knife at Shido, twisting it as she went to dig deep into his side.

"Gah?!"

He felt an intense pain bloom there, and sparks shot across his field of vision.

But Shido didn't fall.

"Stay out of my waaaaay!"

He stilled his shaking fingers, and when the Wizard drew near, he cracked her on the head with the pommel of his sword. Although it wasn't the blade, the Angel itself was a mass of Spirit power. Sandalphon and Territory met with a burst of lightning.

"Wha—!" The Wizard had apparently not expected this. She cried out as she fell.

"Agaah! Unh…" Grimacing and gritting his teeth, Shido pulled the knife out of his side with his free hand. Blood gushed from the open wound, staining the floor around him. The pain that shot through him very nearly made him scream, and he almost passed out.

"Hah!"

But he braced himself, a cold sweat running down his face. He threw the knife, now devoid of magic, to the ground, where it made a clattering sound.

At the same time, a small fire licked at the stab wound. The blessing of the Spirit of flames, Kotori. A healing blaze that automatically patched up his injuries.

But Shido didn't have the luxury of standing there waiting until he was completely healed. He started walking forward again, a searing flame burning on the side of his stomach.

"What on earth is even happening here?" AST captain Ryouko Kusakabe scowled, unable to believe the scene unfolding before her eyes.

Whatever it was, the business district of Kagamiyama was packed with DEM Wizards and mechanical dolls, and countless versions of the Spirit Nightmare all wearing the same face, moving from defense to offense and back as the battle raged.

The sight almost made her forget that this was Japan, and in a sea of office towers on top of that. Bullets flew, magic light flashed, and the orderly rows of buildings were turned into piles of rubble.

After receiving orders to stand by, the AST had finally been given the order to mobilize.

But that order hadn't been to go deal with the Spirit controlling all those people at Tengu Square. Instead, they were to provide backup for DEM because a new Spirit had shown up and was attacking DEM's Japan office.

They were ignoring the unprecedented riot at Tengu Square to respond to the request of a favored supplier. Ryouko had some objections to the priorities on display here, but nevertheless, if there was a new Spirit in play, she couldn't exactly let the havoc unfold unchecked. Ryouko hurried with her team to the business district of Kagamiyama and the DEM Japan office.

She took a deep breath to get herself back on track and started giving instructions.

"All personnel, provide support for the DEM Industries Wizards and eliminate the Nightmare on the ground... It's not an interesting mission, but those are our orders. So get out there and do your jobs."

"Yes sir!"

The AST members in their CR units leaped into the air.

As for Ryouko herself, she would have been lying if she said she trusted DEM. Not only had they forced ten new members onto her team against her will, but they had attempted to do battle in a public place with the general population not evacuated.

That said, however, given that these orders had come down from the highest brass, she didn't have much choice about obeying them. If she let her emotions take over and stepped out of line here, she would be giving the brass an excuse for axing the AST. In the worst case, it was even possible that they would hand the members of the AST over to the DEM Wizards.

And there was also the matter of Origami. Although her conduct had been a clear violation of orders, the danger Squad 3's mission posed was also evident. Ryouko was using that fact as a weapon to reduce the disciplinary action Origami would be facing. She couldn't create any weaknesses in her case now.

Ryouko fired up her thrusters and threw herself into the thick of the melee with the rest of her team. With the enhanced vision her Territory offered her, she picked out one of the several silhouettes flying around in the raging flames and gunpowder smoke, and pulled the trigger on her laser cannon.

"Kee-hee! Hee-hee-hee-hee-hee-hee!"

But Nightmare easily dodged the blast, and instead of counter-attacking, she went off somewhere, making silly gestures as she left. She looked almost as if she were playing.

"What is with them? What on earth do they want?"

And then she heard a strange sound and arched an eyebrow.

"Huh?"

The roar was like standing in the middle of an intense typhoon. She thought maybe it was a plane, but she couldn't see anything like that in the sky. And as a general rule, aircraft other than SDF machines were prohibited from flying through areas with an active spacequake alert.

An instant later, something that she could only describe as a hurricane with a will of its own whipped past, kicking up fierce winds as it cut across her field of vision.

"Wha...!"

She automatically increased the density of her Territory. Blown back by this mass of wind, a number of the Wizards, dolls, and Nightmares lost their balance and tumbled backward.

"Wh-what was that..." She blinked rapidly. She hadn't been able to get a good look at the abrupt phenomenon.

But shadow bullets were closing in on her from below, and Ryouko turned her mind back to the battlefield. The increased density of her Territory repelled the bullets, and she glared at the ground while she readied her laser cannon.

She was curious about the true nature of that hurricane flash, but dealing with Nightmare took priority at the moment. Ryouko fired her thrusters and dove back into the melee between Wizards and Spirit.

"Ngah...!"

It felt like something was shredding the tissues of his muscles in the hand that held Sandalphon. And then a fiery heat assaulted his arm, and he very nearly dropped the sword. But the tendons in his poor hand were healed in the nick of time.

Shido kept fighting to take down the Wizards somehow and move forward in the building, forcibly healing the physical damage from handling Sandalphon with the blessing of Kotori.

He was forcing a power beyond human potential to yield to him by using a power that existed in a realm beyond human knowledge.

But there was no way his human body could endure this cruel cycle indefinitely. The Wizards kept coming, and the healing flames gradually lost ground, unable to keep up with all the damage the Angel was doing to him, until at last, he ended up with his back against the wall.

"Ngh…"

He didn't have the strength left in his arms to raise Sandalphon. He was barely even holding on to the sword, and yet the bones and muscles of his entire body shrieked in agony.

Shido gritted his teeth and looked around.

Three Wizards with guns at the ready. Coming up behind them, another five Wizards. A total of eight human beings surrounded Shido.

"You've given us a bit of trouble, hm? But it's over," one Wizard said, holding up her gun.

Shido suddenly felt like he couldn't breathe.

"Ah! Gah…!"

Most likely, the Wizard was blocking his nose and mouth with her Territory. Or else lowering the concentration of oxygen around him. Apparently, an ordinary human was easy pickings for a Wizard at close range.

He tried to fight, but his legs and arms were very heavy, and he dropped to his knees.

"Ngh! Aah! Aah!"

His vision blurred, and his mind grew hazy.

"Toh…ka…"

But just when he was about to be swallowed by the encroaching darkness, he heard the wall behind him cracking, and in the next instant, the windows lining the corridor shattered. Pieces of glass rained down on their heads.

"Whoa!"

The Wizards were stunned.

But that wasn't the end of the weirdness. A powerful wind rushed in through the broken windows and lifted the three Wizards helplessly into the air.

"Wha...?! M-my Territory, it's—"

Shido felt the temperature around him drop abruptly. It was as if he were suddenly inside a refrigerator.

And it seemed that this was not a hallucination produced by his fading consciousness. He could hear the Wizards ahead of him screaming.

"Th-this..."

"My Territory's freezing?! R-release your Territory now!"

"R-roger!"

The pressure bearing down on him and his trouble breathing vanished as if they had never been.

"Huh?" Blinking rapidly, he looked around at a corridor that was transformed from mere seconds earlier.

The Wizards were panicking. Windows overhead had shattered, and they were being attacked by waves of cold. They were still looking at Shido threateningly, but it was clear they had no clue what was going on.

Soon, however, Shido at least understood everything.

"Hmph. Hoooow pathetic." Miku stepped through a broken window into the corridor, dressed in her shining Astral Dress. At the same time, she did a little dance. "Gabriel. Solo!"

A long, slender silver cylinder appeared. It was apparently one part of that massive pipe organ. The tip of the silver pipe bent in Miku's direction.

It looked exactly like a mic stand.

"—!"

Miku turned toward it, and the voice she produced was so beautiful that anyone would automatically listen in ecstasy.

It passed through the cylinder and reverberated multiple times, spreading out far and wide.

Hearing this song, the Wizards dropped their weapons as one and formed a neat line against the wall.

"Miku!" Shido shouted.

Miku averted her eyes with a displeased sniff. "Could you please not say my name so casually? When my adorable name is spoken with that voice coming from your throat and shaped by your tongue, an iiiiinescapable filth builds up on it."

As always, the pointed verbal abuse seemed incredibly out of place when it came from her charming face, and her words gouged Shido's soul.

He looked out the window to see Yoshino and the Yamai sisters with their Angels manifested. They had likely carried Miku up to this floor of the building.

"Miss Miku...what shall we do?" Yoshino asked, clinging to the back of a giant rabbit doll, and the stern face that Miku had turned toward Shido changed to a smile in an instant as she looked at Yoshino.

"Mm-hmm, riiiight. It seems it'd be a tight squeeze for you and your Angels inside the building... Okay. Please take caaare of the Wizards outside so that no one comes inside to disturb us." Miku held up a finger and winked.

"Keh-keh, indeed. We shall ensure that our Lady Miku's road home is swept clean."

"Concern. Will you be all right without us?"

"Ha-ha-ha!" Miku laughed merrily. "However strong they might be, they're still human beings in the end, yes? There's no way they could eeever get the jump on me, a Spirit!"

The three Spirits looked at one another and nodded.

"If you say so, then..."

"A-accepted! Trust in us to handle this. I vow that we will lay out a velvet carpet directly from this building!"

"Roger. It shall be as you wish, Miss Miku."

"H-hey, Yoshino! Kaguya! Yuzuru!" Shido shouted, but the three Spirits ignored him and flew off in their own directions, spurring their Angels on.

A few seconds later, he saw an icy current of cold air and a mass of wind stir up the Wizard-Kurumi battlefield.

After seeing them off with a satisfied look, Miku turned toward Shido.

"Miku... Why are you—," he started, and then his eyes flew open in surprise. "Are you actually keeping your promise?"

"...!"

She scowled.

"Could you pleaaase not get the wrong idea? I do not care in the sliiiiiiiightest about some unpleasant suicidal jerk blathering on and on about random nonsense in a shrill little voice that's hard on the ears. I came because I wanted to add another Spirit to my collection!"

"Miku," he murmured, and bowed his head. "Thanks. I owe you!"

"Hmph! I *told* you, there's nothing for you to be thaaanking me for. I came of my own will to take Tohka away... You're free to tag along if you must, but please ensure that you stay oooout of my line of sight."

She glanced at him before walking briskly down the hallway, and he hurried after her.

Chapter 9
Demon King

Countless micro missiles filled Mana's field of vision.

Naturally, this many projectiles in an airspace packed with this many people meant that it wouldn't only be the target who took damage. Missiles hit the DEM Wizards and Bandersnatches, and they fell to the ground.

"Those are your allies!" Mana protested.

"Ha-ha-ha-ha-ha! You don't have a chance!" Jessica laughed shrilly, encased inside a massive piece of red machinery.

"It seems...you haven't got any proper judgment left in your head." Mana frowned as she fired her thrusters incrementally to zigzag through the sky.

Each and every blow was a hard one. If she let down her guard for even an instant, she worried that her own Territory could be violated by the powerfully concentrated magic contained in every missile, every gun blast, every swing of the laser blade.

She was certain that Jessica's brain had undergone some kind of magical processing. The same sort of operation that had been done to Mana's body over the course of years, except within the span of hours.

"Ngh—"

She didn't know what exactly they could have done to Jessica to give her this much more strength in less than a day. But it was easy to imagine that, whatever it was, the effect on the body of the warrior would have been profound.

In fact, she could already see the impact in Jessica's actions. The Wizard must have been having trouble thinking clearly because she was so focused on defeating Mana that she was firing her weapons indiscriminately with no regard for the damage she was doing to her own allies. She had even blown up one of the towering DEM facilities in the area.

"Ngh—"

"*Mana! We got your back! Evasive action!*" Kotori's voice rang out through her earpiece.

In the next instant, a small Territory popped into existence. The missiles chasing Mana slammed into this and exploded in midair. The blast triggered several of the other missiles in the dense cluster to also explode. A burst of intense light radiated outward, like fireworks scorching the night sky.

Kotori sent an Yggdrafolium this way and turned it into a mine to defend Mana from the missiles.

"Thanks. You saved me—," she started, but then cut herself off and whirled around.

A current of cold air shot past the space where she had just been.

"This is…!"

For a moment, Mana thought that Jessica had fired a magic cannon, too stubborn to learn her lesson, but that wasn't it. She turned her gaze directly downward and saw a little girl in a maid uniform clinging to an enormous stuffed rabbit.

"Hermit—I mean, Yoshino?!" she cried.

"This is…Miss Miku's order," Yoshino said. "I'll take out…all the Wizards!"

"*Yaah! That's the spirit, Yoshino! Woh-kay! Let's freeze her up nice and good!*"

"Okay…!"

Yoshino exchanged a few words with the rabbit Zadkiel, and then they danced up into the sky while Yoshino pulled icicles out of the air and shot them at Mana.

"Hey!" Mana hurriedly twisted around, and dodged some of the chunks of ice and knocked others to the ground with her laser edge as she raced through the air.

But an incredible wind pressure slammed into her from above, blocking her way forward. Mana frowned, changed her Territory to defensive mode, broke through the wall of wind, and flew up higher.

"Keh-keh! Well then, you do have some skill! So you are unlike these mediocre Wizards crawling around this enclave?"

"Caution. Kaguya, be careful. I believe that is Shido's sister. I've heard she is quite good."

The twin girls, one clutching a lance, the other a pendulum, stared at Mana, their guards up.

"The Yamai sisters...is it?" Mana said, and licked her lips. She tasted a little sweat.

Now that she was thinking about it, these Spirits were also under the control of the Spirit Diva. She'd heard that the *Fraxinus* radar had picked up a wind that seemed to be the Yamai sisters heading for Building 1, but it looked like Yoshino had also tagged along.

She didn't know what they were doing here. But she didn't have the luxury of figuring that out now. While she was dealing with these newcomers, a red silhouette was closing in on her, cutting through the missile blast.

"Seriously?!"

An ordinary opponent would have been one thing, but Jessica's brain had been recklessly toyed with to increase her magical power to the point where she rivaled Mana. Add three Spirits to the mix, and it would be a difficult battle even for a strong fighter like Mana.

"Ngh!" Mana frowned. "Doesn't look like I'll be able to shake off Jessica. I'll have to divert the attention of the Spirits somewhere else!"

She spotted a group of Wizards in the sky ahead. They weren't wearing DEM wiring suits. They were probably the SDF's AST, called in for backup.

"Ah!" She spotted a familiar face among them, and her eyes opened wide in surprise. "Captain!"

"Huh? Y-you—Mana?!" AST Captain Ryouko Kusakabe stared back at Mana with a shocked look on her face. "What on earth are you doing—"

"We'll talk later!" Mana interrupted her. "Tag!"

"Huh?" Ryouko arched an eyebrow at her.

"Take care of these girls!" Mana yelled, and fired her thrusters to race past the AST group.

Rattled by this sudden move, the AST members looked at one another in confusion.

But they were completely taken by surprise a heartbeat later. And that was only natural. Because Hermit and Berserk were charging straight at them.

"Wh-whoa?! All hands! Combat! Squad A, you take Hermit! Squad B, Berserk!"

"R-roger!"

But Ryouko was a captain to her core. She responded to even the most sudden events with a cool head and set about counterattacking the three Spirits.

Yoshino, Kaguya, and Yuzuru noticed this new threat and shifted their target from Mana to the AST. Mana watched this out of the corner of her eye and broke away from that region of the sky.

But she didn't have the chance to even breathe a sigh of relief. All she'd done was maintain the status quo in a situation that threatened to take a turn for the very worst.

Chasing after her from behind, Jessica didn't so much as glance at the Spirits or the AST as she turned her massive magic cannons toward Mana.

"Maaaaanaaaaaaaaa!"

"So stubborn!" Mana scowled and clicked her tongue once more.

And then she felt something like a cold finger running up her spine.

"—?!"

For a second, she thought maybe Yoshino or the Yamai sisters had come after her. But that wasn't the case. This was the sensation when two Territories ate into each other as they overlapped, when two Wizards with Territories deployed over a wide range came into contact.

"Ngh!" Mana hurriedly flipped around and took evasive action.

In the next instant, a laser blade as long as Mana was tall sliced through the space where her body had just been.

"Oh-ho! So you were able to dodge? You have excellent reactions." The girl that had appeared out of nowhere behind Mana raised her chin in a leisurely greeting.

The golden hair dancing in the air, blue eyes. Platinum CR unit over pale skin. DEM Industries' most powerful Wizard, Ellen M. Mathers.

Mana gasped. "Ellen!"

"I heard that there was a big rat among the attackers. So it was you, Mana?" Ellen said, looking down on her. "It's unfortunate. I had viewed you as someone with strength second only to my own at DEM."

"Ha! What a joke," Mana spat. "You're all just messing with people's bodies."

Ellen's eyebrow twitched. "I see. You've learned that much then, have you? It appears that it is true that Ratatoskr took you in."

"Hmph. I'm guessing from the way you're acting that you were in on it, too," Mana replied. "Although the ideal sitch here would have been for you to have a big old change of heart after learning the truth and come with me to give the president a real good thrashing."

"Unfortunately for you, I could never betray Ike."

"Guess not," Mana muttered in annoyance and frowned.

If she was being perfectly honest, this was one woman she didn't want to take on. The pinnacle of the Adeptus Numbers. The world's most powerful Wizard recognized by both herself and everyone else. Although Mana was wearing the Ratatoskr CR unit Vanargand, that was no guarantee she could beat Ellen. And on top of that...

"Go to hell! Blast Arc!" Jessica shouted and launched powerful streams of magic from the two cannons she had turned toward Mana.

"Ngh...!" Mana might have had her Territory, but if she took a direct hit from Licorice cannons, she wouldn't escape unscathed. She twisted around to minimize the impact, so that the blasts slid across the surface of her Territory, then she leaped back so that she could keep both Ellen and Jessica in her sights.

On the right, the most powerful Wizard, clad in platinum armor.

On the left, the most crazed Wizard, carrying a crimson tank on her back.

"I find pitting two against one to be a bit deflating, but well, if that's what Ike wants, then I suppose I will have to oblige. We'll end this quickly."

"Ha! Ha-ha-ha-ha! Mana, looks like you're finally backed into a corner. Maaaanaaaaa?"

"Tsk…"

Mana clicked her tongue in open frustration as not one but two hostile sets of eyes homed in on her.

"So then wheeere is Tohka?" Miku asked as they walked down the hallway. "It's a waste of time to go charging around this big building at random."

"Oh. Uh," Shido said awkwardly. It wasn't like he knew her exact location.

"What?" Miku frowned. "Did you break in here without inveeeestigating? Hm? Is that ugly lump sitting on your shoulders like a clay doll stuffed with overboiled udon noodles?"

"Hngh…" Bull's-eye. He began to stammer, "B-but it's not so easy to find stuff like that out!"

"Hmm. Do you reeeally think so?" She stopped, heels clacking against the floor, and looked over the DEM Wizards lined up against the wall after hearing her song. She selected the youngest girl from among them and crooked her finger at her. "You there. Please come over here!"

"Y-yes, Miss Miku!" The girl walked over to Miku nervously.

Miku lifted her chin with a charming gesture. "Say? Please do tell me. Where is Tohka looocked up?"

"Th-that's…confidential…"

"If you don't tell me, I'll hate you, you know?" Miku said, a smile flitting across her face.

"N-no! Miss Miku!" The Wizard's face crumpled like she was about to burst into tears as she clung to Miku. "She's in the isolation area on the eighteenth floor! Y-you can use this ID to get inside! P-please, Miss Miku! Have mercy! Please!"

"Hee-hee-hee! I adooore obedient girls!" Miku took the ID card, brought her index finger to her lips, and then touched it to the girl's.

"A-aah?!" The girl let out an ecstatic cry and dropped lifelessly to the ground. It seemed the rush of emotions was simply too much for her mind to bear.

The other Wizards fidgeted jealously and yanked on imaginary handkerchiefs. Even the men were doing it, so the whole scene was just a little surreal.

But Miku paid no attention to these believers. Instead, she turned contemptuous eyes on Shido, a victorious look on her face. "How do you like that? There are aaaall kinds of ways, you know?"

"...Apologies." Normally, he would have rebuked Miku for recklessly toying with human beings, like she had at the Tenou Festival, but the situation they were currently facing called for some drastic action. He scratched his cheek, a complicated mix of emotion in his heart.

But at least they had gotten both Tohka's location and the key to getting inside. He clenched his fists and turned his gaze toward the upper floors.

"All right. Let's go, Miku."

"Could you pleeeease not make it feel like we're working together?" she demanded. "You do understand, yes? I simply want to add Tohka to my army. You and I are enemies!"

"I-I get it." He had a few things he would have liked to say, but the fact was, without Miku, he wouldn't have even known where Tohka was. He simply followed meekly when she began to walk again.

Who knew how many stairs they had climbed or how far they had walked when they spotted another group of Wizards in wiring suits, equipped with close-range weapons and small arms. They had likely been informed of the irregularity that was Miku. They were better equipped than the Wizards Shido had faced alone, and their faces were tense.

"Fire! Show no mercy!" a Wizard said, apparently the squad leader, and the Wizards opened fire.

Miku took a deep breath.

"Wah!"

The sound she produced was substantial and formed a barrier in front of her.

The bullets closing in on Miku and Shido were repelled by the invisible wall of sound and sank into the floor and the surrounding walls. The Wizards cried out in confusion. Although the wall of sound had a directionality, the shaking of the air still reached Shido, and he unconsciously plugged his ears.

"Ha-ha-ha!" Miku laughed. "Were you trying to stop meeeee with an attack like that? You've really underestimated me, hm?"

The faces of the Wizards twisted in fear.

And then two more Wizards showed up in the corridor behind them, pistols aimed squarely at Miku's back.

"Miku!" Shido shouted, and swung Sandalphon with both hands.

The light from the blade flew out in the arc of the sword and sent the Wizards and their Territories sailing backward. The bullets fired from their guns were knocked up into the ceiling.

"Ngah!"

An intense pain raced through Shido's body, originating in the hands that held the sword. He dropped to his knees.

"Hngh…!"

"H-hey?!" Miku called to him with a frown, having cleared away the Wizards ahead of them.

But Shido didn't even have the strength to respond to her.

This Spirit sword was more than a human body could handle, and the price he paid for swinging it again and again and again was higher than he'd anticipated. The burden of commanding the Angel ate into his flesh, and he felt as if needles were shooting out of every bone in his body and ripping open his flesh from the inside.

But the power of Kotori that lived inside him hadn't abandoned him yet. He felt a fiery heat grow in the depths of his heart and gradually spread out to his extremities. He could tell that the flames were healing the invisible damage to his muscles, bones, and organs. Of course, this violent remedy was accompanied by a hellish heat.

"Unh! Ngh!"

Still, he couldn't complain. He gritted his teeth against the pain, which nearly sent his consciousness into a black void, and stood up. He somehow managed to start walking again, dragging the tip of Sandalphon along the floor.

Miku sniffed in annoyance. "How unsightly. Why would you push yourself so haaaard?"

"I told you... I have to rescue Tohka. Who knows what they're doing to her while I'm here wasting time on my ass... I can't stay here," he said, clenching a fist and wincing at the pain of that. "Ngh..."

"Aah, aah, aah." Miku arched an eyebrow and then deliberately filled her face with loathing. "How terribly cold. What is this about? Are you drunk on the idea of rescuing the traaaaagic heroine? You're much too old to dream of being a hero."

Miku shrugged scornfully and continued.

"Ah-ha-ha! Is that maybe it? You said before that Tohka was more important than your own life, so you've gone toooo far to back down now? It's fine, really. I am well aware of the ugliness of human beings, so I won't be disappointed if you walk away now."

"..."

But Shido simply walked silently down the corridor.

"Hey! Are you ignoooring me?!" Not particularly caring for this, Miku chased after Shido, and then slapped a fist in one hand as though a thought had just occurred to her. "Ohh, I know. How about we do this then? Please say that you give up on Tohka. If you do, I'll use my voice to make howeeeeever many girls you like your slaves. What do you think? They'll obey you absolutely. They'll do aaaanything for you, you know? Hee-hee-hee! That's not such a bad deal, hm?"

Shido's eyebrows shot up.

The whole thing left an unpleasant taste in his mouth. It wasn't to his advantage to put Miku in a bad mood. He was only too well aware of this, but he still couldn't let this pass without speaking his mind. He glared at her sternly.

"You can't be serious? There's no replacement for Tohka!"

Miku jumped a little before speaking again, her voice angry. "H-hmph! How long are you going to put on this little show?! After all, that's about all your talk about love and how important someone is amounts to, right? I'm telling you I'll find you a replacement, so that should be fine for you! Why would you go to such lengths?!"

Her tone grew more forceful. If she was just trying to lead Shido astray, it was a bit much. She sounded almost like the fact that Shido was not taking her up on this offer was a rejection of her very self.

"You've got the wrong idea," he told her. "Human beings aren't all like tha—"

"Shut! Uuuuuuup!" Miku shouted. "Human beings are my playthings! Boys are slaves! Girls are cute dolls! Human beings have no other value!"

"Miku, you..." Shido furrowed his brow. The words he didn't get to ask inside Kurumi's shadows popped back up in his mind. "Why... why do you hate men so much? Why do you treat girls like things? Why do you see human beings like this?!"

"Ha! That's obvious, isn't it? Human beings are just that—"

"But *you're* human!"

Shido cut her off.

"—?!"

She gasped and turned stunned eyes on him.

He met her gaze and continued. "You used to be a human being, and then Phantom—a *something* made out of static—gave you Spirit powers. Am I wrong?!"

"...!"

Miku's shoulders jumped up. But she didn't deny it.

This was what Kurumi had shared with him on the way to DEM. This was the information she had read from the items they found in Miku's house—the CDs that had been published under a different name and a photo of a young Miku with what appeared to be her parents.

Just like Kotori, Miku was a human being who had been turned into a Spirit. And she had performed as an idol under a different name before that happened.

"How do you know that?" Miku glared at him with sharp eyes.

This was all the response he needed.

"Got it from an acquaintance." Shido dodged the question with a vague answer. There was no need to get into all the things Kurumi could do.

But he didn't actually know the whole story. Much of the information Kurumi got from the photo and the CDs was fragmented. There was still plenty he didn't understand about Miku.

Like how if she had originally been human, then why did she treat other human beings like objects?

It wasn't only that she hated men. She interacted with the girls she liked as though she were playing with delicate antique dolls. She didn't treat human beings as living creatures like herself. This felt so powerfully wrong to him.

Shido had thought that Miku's values were warped because she had been born with this voice and the power to make anyone do anything.

But if she had been human...

If she had lived in human society for a decade or more...

...What on earth had happened to make her feel so disconnected from human beings?

"You're human, too. So then you should—," he started, and Miku glared at him with sharp eyes.

"Please don't be ridiiiiculous!" she shouted hatefully. "How could you... What do *you* know?!"

Shido opened his mouth slowly. "Miku... What happened to you?"

"Hmph! Why would I—"

"Miku," he said, pressing her, and she sighed in sheer annoyance.

"You're soooo persistent. Hmph."

Miku began to talk, practically spitting the words out.

All I have is singing.

Miku had already realized this at the age of nine.

When it came to school and sports, it was faster to count her rank from the bottom. She wasn't good at art or making things, either. Not one of her elementary school report cards had a single "well done," and that fact didn't change when she moved on to junior high school.

But she had her voice. She could sing beautifully, better than anyone else in her class.

When had it started... Oh, yes. Her kindergarten sports meet. Her teacher had complimented her, telling her that she was such a good singer.

This made little Miku very happy. She felt proud, as if she had been given a shiny medal no one else had.

It was perhaps a foregone conclusion that she began to dream of being one of the idols who sang and danced on TV.

Young Miku became utterly engrossed with those girls and their adorable voices, dancing on the glittering stage. She memorized not only the lyrics of their songs but the choreography of their dances as well, mimicking them so perfectly that even her parents were surprised.

And then when Miku was fifteen, she caught the eye of the judges at an audition and made her long-awaited debut as an idol under the name Tsukino Yoimachi.

The joy she felt was indescribable. After dreaming of it for so many years, she was finally right where she wanted to be. Now so, so many people would hear her voice and her songs. Just the thought of it was enough to make tears spill from her eyes.

Although she was nothing then compared to how she was now, her career went very smoothly, no obstacles popped up to hold her back. Her CDs climbed the charts, and the crowds at her concerts grew bigger and bigger. Her audience was more than 90 percent male, a sight which made her shiver with repulsion when she thought about it now. But to Miku back then, they were her precious fans, people who swore they loved her singing with all their heart.

She liked recording CDs and radio performances well enough, but she really did have the most fun with her concerts. That's when she felt most keenly that her song was reaching all these people.

Everyone complimented her singing. They said they loved her.

The shiny medal pinned to her chest gleamed even more beautifully. She thought she would live this dream forever.

But the end came surprisingly soon and with little fanfare.

About a year after Miku made her debut, just when she was hitting her stride and getting a serious fanbase, her manager at the talent agency told her that a certain TV producer had taken a liking to her. If she *played nice* with him, she could get a regular spot on a prime-time show or something.

Although no one spelled it out for her, she knew it was basically *that* sort of thing.

Naturally, she politely refused. She hadn't become an idol so she could be on TV; she'd wanted everyone to hear her singing.

But soon after, a weekly photo magazine printed some alleged scandal she knew nothing about.

What was it again? She had been too shocked to actually read all the details, but she did remember that it was the kind of thing that would raise eyebrows—a past relationship, an abortion, hanging out with drug dealers—something of the sort.

She learned later that the producer in question had been a part of it. He also happened to be quite chummy with the president of Miku's agency. And just like that, Miku was dropped by her manager.

But the hardest part of it all had been the reaction of her fans— no, the people she'd *thought* were her fans. The people who told her "You're the best," "I love you," "I could die for you," etc., etc. Their attitudes changed overnight.

It was painful that they would believe some random stranger over Miku.

Hey, how many times did you do it with your ex?

An abortion? So you basically killed a baby. What are you even doing here, you murderer?

Every time a comment like this popped up on her blog, every time someone said something cruel to her at the handshake events and signings, which drew fewer and fewer attendees every time, a part of her heart was gouged out.

She didn't give up, though. She still had her songs. She had her singing. Right from the beginning, that was all she'd ever had.

Whatever rumors people spread, she was sure they'd understand the truth once they heard her singing.

There's power in my songs.

This baseless conviction remained somewhere in her heart.

And so Miku stood onstage once more.

But it was awful.

The people crowded into the venue looked like terrifying beasts, different from herself somehow, and her heart pounded with something other than nervous tension.

But she had to sing. Nothing would start unless she sang.

The music began. She brought her mouth to the mic. She strained her vocal cords.

However.

…! …!

Only wheezing came out of her mouth.

Later, she went to the hospital and was diagnosed with psychogenic dysphonia.

Thus, the life of Tsukino Yoimachi came to its swift end. If a girl who had nothing but singing lost her voice, then that girl's existence had no value. She had known that for a long time. She had already understood it when she was nine.

That was when Miku started to think about suicide.

Any method would have been fine. Hanging herself. An overdose of

sleeping pills. She could also jump in front of a train, and she didn't mind simply putting her hand on a razor blade and pulling. A simple movement to quickly dispose of a girl with no value.

But when Miku was about to actually do it, God came to her.

"You, disappointed by humanity. You, despairing of the world. Don't you want power? Don't you want a lot of power, enough to change the whole world?"

"I lost it. Once. With the psychogenic dysphonia, because of those ugly men. My voice... More precious than life itself, my voice...!" Miku cried out, like she was about to burst into tears right then and there. "I thought about killing myself a million times. But then God came to me and gave me this voice! The most powerful voice! To make people my slaves with each and every song!"

Most likely, this "God" was the same mysterious Spirit Phantom who gave Kotori her Spirit powers.

"Is that what happened?" Shido said.

He felt an absurd disconnect from this Miku who didn't treat people like people. He felt like her values, her view of life and death, were simply too far removed from human beings. To the point where he'd even felt rage at it.

When he found the CDs and photo at her house and realized that Miku might have had a past as a human being, that disconnect had grown even more pronounced.

But he understood now.

Naturally, he did not in any way approve of how Miku interacted with people. He really couldn't accept her way of doing things, of acting like a queen and enslaving everyone around her with a voice imbued with Spirit power.

But he understood now. It wasn't that Miku thought of human beings as inferior to herself.

She was so scared, so terribly frightened of interacting with them as an equal. If she trusted them, they would betray her. If she opened herself up to them, they would abandon her. If she relied on them, they would deceive her.

If that was how it would be, then she would simply expect nothing. Distancing herself from human beings was the natural choice. She had to constantly keep in mind that humans were a different species. No matter what happened, she would never give herself over to a human being.

This was her unconscious defense mechanism, and it stemmed from losing her precious voice once before because of the despair other human beings had made her feel.

The producer who tortured her with a fabricated scandal because she wouldn't be his, the fans who hurt her, made to dance to the pro-ducer's tune—she scorned and rejected these selfish men.

But she was unable to open up to women, either. She no longer inter-acted with them as anything other than adorable dolls who would never betray her.

"That's why I hate men! They're despicable, dirty, ugly. Just looking at one makes me want to vomit!" Miku spat. "And yes, with girls! As long as there are cute girls who will do as I say, I don't need anything else! All those other humans can just drop dead for all I care!"

"...!"

Shido gasped. He did understand Miku's suffering. Losing her all-important voice must have been very hard indeed.

But...

"You're wrong! I do think what happened to you was terrible! That producer and whoever wrote that article about you make me furious! And I'm angry at the fans who turned on you, too! But you can't go hating all the other human beings along with them!"

"What?! Be quiet! All men are exactly the same!"

"No, let me talk!" he shouted back. "Was there really not a single per-son who listened to your singing? I mean, weren't there people who weren't swayed by the scandal, who were really excited to see you sing?!"

"H-how could there—!"

They heard footfalls echoing ahead in the corridor. Wizards with pistols at the ready soon appeared.

"There they are! The intruders!"

"Be careful! One of them's a Spirit!"

"...!"

Shido gasped and readied Sandalphon in his hands. Kotori's flames had apparently healed his body enough for him to swing the blade again. Although he was still in pain, it wasn't so bad that it knocked him off his feet.

He glanced over at Miku.

They had to defeat these Wizards. But this was the first time Miku had opened up about her past. If he let this opportunity get away, he had the feeling he'd be back at square one.

The Wizards fired in unison. But their bullets were repelled by Miku's wall of sound.

Aiming for this opening, Shido's sword flashed and he shouted, "Miku! You've created this terrifying phantom of human beings in your mind! And you make everyone do what you want with that voice, so this phantom just keeps getting bigger! And you get more and more afraid of talking with a real person!"

"Huh?!" Miku cried out in disbelief. "Scared? How dare you?! You're saying I'm *afraid* of people?! And we're in the middle of battle, you know? Don't go getting—Aaaah!"

The Wizards' bullets closed in on them. When Miku raised her voice at Shido, she created a wall of sound at the same time and knocked the projectiles away.

"Like that's got anything to do with this!" he snapped back. "I'll say it however many times you want! You've been surrounded by nothing but yes-people this whole time because you're afraid to have a conversation with a real human being! But even though you reject people, somewhere in your heart, what you really want is to talk to someone!"

"What slander!" she said. "What would someone like you know about that?!"

Shido swung Sandalphon, and together they knocked back the Wizards that appeared and made their way down the corridor.

"I *know*! I mean, isn't that why you wanted a person you couldn't control with your voice? Isn't that why you wanted Shiori Itsuka?!"

"...!"

Miku gasped, and twisted her face up.

Yes. She said she only needed people who did what she told them to, but she had been fixated by the anomaly that was Shiori.

"Th-that's simply—," she protested.

"And when you made your debut again with this new voice, you didn't go with Tsukino Yoimachi or some new stage name!" Shido shouted. "You used your real name, Miku Izayoi, right? You...you wanted people to know you, didn't you? You were saying, *I'm right here!* You wanted people to approve of you, didn't you?! You wanted that from none other than these human beings!"

Miku clenched her teeth, and her face was dyed red. "Shut. Uuuuuuuuuuuup!" she shrieked. "Shut it shut it shut iiiiit! Talking like you know anything! Stupid! Idiot! You morooooon!"

The last part was nothing but insults. But her voice apparently carried some potent Spirit power nonetheless. Wizards up ahead poked their faces out and were pushed back by an invisible wall.

"H-hey! So I poke a sore spot and you—"

"As if you could ever bother me! You're wrong! You're just an idiot! Idiot! Idiot! Idiot!"

"Aaaaah! Come *on*! I can't let you have Yoshino, Kaguya, and Yuzuru! I am absolutely going to seal your Spirit power!" he shouted, and Miku's shoulders jumped up.

"I will...*never* let you do that! If you seal this voice, then I'll—" Miku gritted her teeth and then continued. "You... You're telling me to be that?! A me without song... A me without value!"

"That's *not* what I'm saying!" He swung the Angel through the air. The sword strike became light and slashed through the Wizards' Territories. "I...I just want you to sing in your real voice, the one without the power to enslave people!"

This was how he really felt. He had heard her human voice at the Izayoi house. It was full of an earnest appeal her voice now lacked.

However.

Miku twisted up her face in displeasure. "Please don't talk as though you know anything! It's because I have this voice that I can be a top idol! Who exactly would want to listen to my singing without this voice?!"

"*I* would!" he yelled.

Miku's eyes flew open, a shudder running through her body. "Wh-what... You're all talk! You've never even heard my singing!"

"I have! Just one song!" he told her. "It was earnest and intent and cool! I liked it far better than the way you sing now! No one would listen to your singing? Ha! Don't be ridiculous. At the very least, whatever happens, you've got one fan who's not going anywhere! He's right here!"

"Wha..."

"Spirit power's got nothing to do with it. Even without that voice, you're not worthless! Not by a long shot!"

"...!!"

Now Miku looked like she was about to cry. But she quickly sniffed contemptuously, as if she had rethought the situation.

"I...I don't believe you! All the fans who said that, none of them believed in me! When I was having a hard time...none of them reached out to me!"

"I don't think that's true," he replied. "I'm sure you had fans who believed in you, who waited for you. But...even if that were true! If you were in trouble, *I* would reach out to you!"

"You're just saying what you think I want to hear to get your own way! So then what? You're saying that if I was in trouble like Tohka is, you'd risk your life to save me or something?!" Miku shouted, glaring at Shido. Like she wanted to watch as he struggled for an answer.

But he spoke up without hesitation. "Of course!"

"...!"

Miku stopped where she stood. And then scowled unhappily and chased after him.

"I don't believe you! It's a lie! It's obviously a lie!"

"Look, you—"

Just then, as they climbed the stairs to the next floor, a Wizard appeared before them. It was a large man. Unlike the other Wizards they'd encountered, his hands held an enormous Gatling gun that was very clearly not intended for indoor combat.

"Halt right there!" he barked. "Looks like you've had the run of the place so far, but that ends here! Charged with protecting the building by Executive Leader Mathers, I, Andrew Carthy Dunsten Francis Barbirolli—"

""Shut up!"" Shido and Miku shouted in unison.

The Gatling gun distorted under the pressure of Miku's voice, and the Wizard's Territory was severed in half with one blow from Sandalphon.

"Ngh! Ah!" Andrew Whatever-it-was yelped and passed out on the spot.

Sounding like she'd done nothing more than kick aside a pebble on the road, Miku continued. "And honestly, why would I even have to be rescued by you anyway?! Please know your limits and your place!"

"Wait! *You're* the one who asked if I'd rescue you!"

"Hmph! I have no idea what you're talking about!" She whirled her face away, and his face tightened.

"You...!"

But then Shido realized that this floor was different from the others. Sturdy walls, not a single window. Almost like—yes, like an isolation facility.

"Hold on... Is this the place?" He furrowed his brow and looked ahead.

And saw a door in one part of the barrier wall that stretched out before them.

"Ngh!"

The situation was less than ideal.

Ellen and Jessica with her enhanced magical processing. Mana was simultaneously facing off against what were likely the two most powerful fighters DEM currently possessed.

Racing through the sky at top speed to try and dodge the cluster of micro missiles advancing on her, Mana checked the positions of her enemies with her Territory. Behind her, Jessica. But she couldn't pick up Ellen's signal.

In the next instant, a Territory touched hers. She reacted quickly and swung the laser edge of her right arm.

Ellen's laser blade came down in that very spot, and a shower of sparks scattered when their weapons collided.

"Ngh!"

"That's quite the reaction speed. But do you really think you can win in combat against me?" Ellen said, and swung her laser blade so fast, it turned into a formless blur.

Mana couldn't follow it with her dynamic vision. Instead, she focused every nerve in her body, increased the precision of her Territory, and swung her laser edge in reaction to the slicing attack that touched her Territory.

But she wasn't up against just one opponent. While Mana fended off Ellen's attacks, Loot Box—Licorice's weapons container—fired another cluster of missiles at her back.

Some of the projectiles exploded before they could reach her. Most likely, *Fraxinus* providing support with Yggdrafolium. But there were just too many of them. The missiles that escaped the blast ripped into her back.

"Hngah!" she groaned.

"Wah-ha-ha-ha-ha! Bull's-eeeeeye! That's a no-noooo! You gotta watch your back, tooooo!"

Jessica's disturbing laughter reached her ears.

Although Mana had her Territory deployed, she had all of its energy turned toward Ellen, and so the invisible barrier wasn't able to completely absorb the impact of the missiles. Her brain rocked inside her head, and she very nearly blacked out.

But Mana bit the inside of her cheek and managed to stay conscious.

She issued orders in her mind, activating her thrusters to try and pull back. She needed a second to regroup.

However.

When she tried to retreat, her path was blocked by an invisible wall.

"Wha...!" Her eyes flew open, and she quickly realized the true nature of the obstruction. A limited Territory generated by Licorice. The Licorice models were able to produce Territories in spaces other than the one occupied by the user.

"Bit soft, aren't yaaaa? It ends here, Manaaaaa!" Jessica laughed, a gruesome smile on her face.

"You...think that's all I've got?!" Mana issued mental orders and knocked Jessica's Territory aside.

But Ellen hadn't let that opening slip past her. A momentarily look of displeasure at the interruption in their battle crossed her face, but she then shook her head to refocus and brandished her laser blade Caledfwlch.

"Hnngh!"

Ellen was too close for Mana to dodge the blow. She switched her Territory to defensive mode and braced herself for the impact.

And then Ellen gasped. "Wha...!" She furrowed her brow doubtfully as a laser cannon blast came squarely at her from the right.

She knocked the magical light away with her raised laser blade, and Mana used this chance to knock Jessica's Territory away and fall back.

"What was that?"

For a second, she thought it was backup from *Fraxinus*, but no. When she turned her eyes in the direction of the cannon blast, she saw a doll-like girl floating there, shoulder-length hair pulled back.

"M-Master Sergeant Tobiichi?!" Mana cried automatically.

Yes. Charging in from outside to sucker punch Ellen was Mana's former colleague, Origami Tobiichi.

"You okay?"

Mana frowned. Something was off here. Origami was wearing a wiring suit and a CR unit, but the design of both was different from standard AST equipment. The navy wiring suit was daringly open in a plunging V down to her navel and a mess of mismatched weapons. It looked like she'd literally grabbed whatever equipment she could get a hold of.

"Origami Tobiichi?" Ellen frowned dubiously. "You should be recovering. And that equipment isn't AST issue..."

Origami ignored her and turned her eyes toward Mana. "Shido?"

"Huh?" Mana said. "My brother? Yes, he's doing all right."

Origami's face relaxed the tiniest bit. "Where is he now?"

"Um, Building One."

"Oh." Origami nodded the tiniest bit, fired her thrusters, and flew off toward Building 1.

But Ellen raced through the sky after her. "Do you think I would just let you go?"

"I'll force my way through."

Origami and Ellen glared at each other, their Territories bumping. Magic rippled outward.

"Master Sergeant Tobiichi!" Mana called, and issued commands in her brain to provide backup for Origami.

The difference in power between Origami and Ellen was obvious. On top of that, Origami couldn't possibly have recovered from the battle the day before so quickly. Origami would be killed.

But when Mana started toward Origami, a blast from a high-output magic cannon shot in front of her, blocking her path. She didn't have to wonder where it came from—Jessica.

"Where are you going? I'm the one you need to concerned abouuuut."

"You...!" Mana scowled and made the laser edge in her hand vibrate.

Origami changed orientation in the sky. Her operation of this unit was still not very steady, likely because she wasn't familiar with it, but she couldn't do anything about that. She reached a hand around behind her and pushed the laser cannon on her back forward.

The wiring suit she was wearing was not procured by the AST, but equipment formally adopted by the SSS—Special Sorcery Services, a British anti-Spirit unit. Additionally, the large laser cannon, the assault rifle loaded with anti-Spirit bullets, the Gatling gun, and the other close-range equipment she had were a mishmash of whatever happened to be on hand.

This was the idea that Mikie had come up with. A CR unit hidden in the basement of an empty apartment building, not managed by IDs. It had been concealed there by a terrorist group made up of former SSS members who had attacked the AST several months earlier. The majority of their equipment had been seized, but it seemed they had kept reserves in the abandoned cache that Mikie discovered.

"...!"

Origami turned her gaze on her opponent, who cut a graceful figure in the air.

The girl pulled back her beautiful blond hair. "Origami Tobiichi. I never imagined I would find you here."

Origami recognized her. This was the photographer who'd come along on their school trip.

When she thought about it, several other parts of that trip were obviously suspect. The sudden change in destination right before their departure, the DEM mechanical dolls that had appeared before Origami.

So when she saw Ellen Mathers attacking Mana, rather than being surprised, she felt things clicking into place.

"I was told that you used Licorice in a fight against Bailey and were unable to do battle after surpassing activation limits. Even if you were treated with a medical Realizer, you can't possibly be well enough to be out of bed, much less wearing a CR unit. I say this with genuine concern—if you push yourself too hard, you will die."

"That's got nothing to do with this."

"I see."

A wiring suit she wasn't accustomed to using, and an assortment of rarely used, outdated equipment, likely concealed from the military. Those were the only cards in Origami's hand. But she could still fight. No matter how despairingly large the difference in strength was, she could turn her sword on her enemy.

She was up against a DEM Wizard in cutting-edge equipment. Origami just might die here. And if she was lucky enough to survive, she might never be able to fight again.

But even if that was the case, she had to save Shido. To this end, she didn't care what kind of surprise moves, what kind of tricks, what kind of coincidences she had to rely on!

Origami noticed the change in the numbers projected onto her retinas and got some distance from Ellen.

The magic values for Ellen's powerful Territory kept going up. This likely meant she was preparing for battle.

But Origami didn't need to see the numbers to know that. She had been able to more or less guess at Ellen's power when she touched her Territory earlier. Ellen was more powerful than Mana, and Mana had wiped the floor with Origami and the rest of the AST during mock battles. Origami had never before touched a Territory with such a dense concentration of magic woven into it. If she were careless enough to engage Ellen at close range, that alone would spell the end of Origami's little excursion.

"...!"

The action her brain decided on was immediate. She fired the anti-Spirit assault rifle in her right hand and the Gatling gun in her left, and pulled the trigger on her laser cannon with her Territory to launch a barrage at Ellen.

She didn't have artillery to spare. In fact, she hadn't even had the Gatling gun in her left hand when she originally set out. She'd grabbed it from a Bandersnatch full of holes on her way here.

But given that she didn't have a chance of winning in close-range combat, her only option was to attack from afar. Absorbing the recoil with her Territory, she concentrated all her magic-imbued bullets on one spot.

Eventually, the rain of bullets ended. Naturally, not because Origami wanted it to stop. She simply ran out of ammunition.

When the curtain of smoke was cleared away by the wind, however, Ellen was floating there leisurely, clad in a CR unit without a scratch on it.

"Did you really think such a thing would be effective?" Ellen sighed, exasperated, and turned the laser blade in her hand toward Origami. "If you did, then you have certainly underestimated me."

But then her eyebrows arched up.

The wall of a building was falling toward her, riddled with holes from Origami's attack.

Naturally, Origami had never thought she could do anything to Ellen with bullets. So she had kept Ellen's focus on her while she worked on the building rising up behind her.

"Hmph." Without even moving, Ellen stopped the massive pile of rubble closing in from above when it was on the verge of touching her head.

But this was also within the realm of expectation. Origami released the connection on the assault rifle in her hand, poured magic into the body of the weapon, and threw it with all her might at Ellen.

Naturally, this was also blocked by Ellen's Territory before it could reach her body. And then something like a gas began to stream from the lower part of the weapon.

"Wha—This is…!" Ellen frowned and covered her mouth with her hand.

Origami had attached a grenade to the rifle and set it so that the pin was pulled when it cleared her Territory.

Still, it wasn't as though the gas itself were a powerful poison. It merely gave off a foul odor and was used to put down riots. At most, it would cause a powerful itching in the eyes and nose.

But Ellen had no way of knowing that. Given that she might have been sprayed with a poisonous gas, she had no choice but to mitigate the potential effects with her Territory, or pull her Territory in tight around her to shut out the gas.

"Now!" Origami pulled a stun grenade from where it hung on her hip and lobbed it at Ellen. There was an intense flash accompanied by an earsplitting *bang*.

Less than a heartbeat later, she issued orders in her mind and shifted to the micro missile pod on her back, launching every single one of them at the more powerful Wizard.

The Territory was maintained by a basic Realizer built into the wiring suit. And that Realizer was controlled by none other than the human brain.

Ellen's brain at the moment would have been carrying out parallel processing to handle a number of issues—defending from the rubble from the building, mitigating the gas, guarding against the light and sound. On top of that, she was being showered in micro missiles processed with magic. If she'd been an average Wizard, her brain would have overheated, and she would have either failed to deal with one of these attacks or released her Territory for a moment.

However...

"You thought this through, hm?"

"...?!"

Origami heard a voice from behind and gasped.

But she was too late. At the same time as she hurriedly whirled around, a hand grabbed her throat. The effect of the Territory holding her body up weakened, and gravity suddenly weighed on her heavily.

"Ngh..."

"Rather than trying to engage the Territory itself, you confuse the brain that generates it. Is that how you managed to do this? I see. It's not a particularly elegant method, but it is effective," Ellen said, having appeared behind Origami at some point, and squeezed the hand around her throat.

"You were so close, hm? You no doubt would have won if your opponent had been anyone other than myself. But unfortunately. This is not a method to be used against the world's most powerful Wizard."

The corners of Ellen's mouth turned up in a smile.

Fifteen thousand meters in the air above DEM's Japan branch, the main monitor on the bridge of *Fraxinus* was showing a video feed of the total chaos unfolding in the business district.

"Wizards approaching Mana's rear! Bearing down at one o'clock!"

"Send out Yggdrafolium 3 and 4."

"Roger. Yggdrafolium 3 and 4 set to land mine mode."

At the same time as the cool voice rang out, a small explosion occurred in the air above the business district on-screen.

"Counterattack confirmed. Target has lost Territory."

Most likely, no one had noticed them in among all the blasts and commotion of the battle, but Kotori and her crew had sent all the autonomous Yggdrafolium units to the ground, where they were providing support for Mana.

As long as they couldn't connect with Shido inside the building, this was about all that they could so. Kotori managed to keep her frustration in check while she dispassionately carried out her work.

"C-Commander! There!" a member of her crew cried out.

Kotori turned her eyes to the monitor and saw the battlefield and two girls hanging in the air. No. Actually, to be more precise, a blond girl in platinum armor had her hand around the neck of a girl in a navy suit and was holding her up midair.

"That's..." Kotori furrowed her brow.

"It appears to be...Ellen Mathers and Origami Tobiichi," Kannazuki said from beside her, putting a finger to his chin.

Yes. Although she was wearing unfamiliar equipment, the girl being strangled was Shido's classmate and AST Wizard Origami Tobiichi.

DEM and the AST were supposedly working together. In fact, the AST had also joined the fray earlier and were fighting the Kurumis alongside the DEM Wizards.

But Kotori quickly reassessed the situation.

She remembered how when a group of unknown AST personnel had appeared in the air above Tengu Square the day before, perhaps targeting a Spirit, Origami had tried to stop them using the weapon of annihilation called White Licorice. It was hard to think that Origami had been acting to protect Tohka and the others, strictly speaking, especially not when she hated Spirits the way she did. The likeliest explanation was that she had wanted to save Shido in Tengu Square.

"It can't be..." Kotori flicked the stick of the Chupa Chups in her mouth up as she stared at the monitor.

She could think of only one reason why Origami was fighting the DEM Wizard right now.

"Prepare the convergent magic power cannon Mistilteinn. We're going to give Origami Tobiichi some backup."

"Are you certain?" Kawagoe asked from the lower deck.

Kotori glanced at him and let out a short sigh. "My feelings here are complicated. I'll have trouble sleeping if I let her be killed. And I can't just walk away from someone who's trying to help Shido, whatever her reasons."

She pulled the lollipop from her mouth and snapped it at the girl in the monitor.

"AR-008, parallel operation of five and six. Commence magic charging. Turn gun number three downward at the same time. Switch partial control to manual. Target: Ellen Mathers," Kotori said.

"But, Commander." Minowa on the lower deck spoke up, a troubled look on her face. "The target is in close proximity to Origami Tobiichi. Even if we curb our output, isn't there a risk of collateral damage?"

It was a reasonable concern. But Kotori snorted in disdain.

"That's why I told you to switch it to partial manual. Kannazuki."

"Yes sir!" Kannazuki nodded.

"Get a headset. I'll leave the targeting to you. You can do it, yes?"

"If you gave the order, I would nail an apple sitting on her head without fail." He bowed his head without an instant of hesitation.

The members of the crew gulped loudly and began to tap at their consoles, following Kotori's orders.

"Now then. The truth is, I enjoy sparring with you, but unfortunately, I am in a hurry myself," Ellen said in a quiet voice, squeezing Origami's neck tightly. She raised the enormous laser blade in her right hand and touched it to the other girl's cheek.

"Unh… Hngh…," Origami groaned.

"You're a favorite of Ike's, and I don't really want to kill you. But it seems you're a clever one, and it would not be to our advantage to simply leave you running free."

She fired up the blade of her sword. Origami heard a sizzling sound and felt a sharp pain on her cheek.

"Ngah!"

And then she saw something flash brightly like a shooting star in the dark sky. Followed by a beam of light cascading down toward them.

"—?!"

"Wha..."

That light shot straight at Ellen, right into the top of her head. The moment it touched her Territory, tiny implosions of magic scattered like sparks.

This was the product of a super-high-energy magic gun on a level that was impossible for an individual's equipment. The pillar of light was probably even more powerful than White Licorice's Blast Arc.

"Wh-what is this?!"

It seemed that even Ellen hadn't been expecting this blow. For the first time, anguish colored her face. And Origami felt the power blocking her Territory weaken, perhaps because Ellen simply couldn't react in time to the blast from nowhere.

"...!"

Taking advantage of the instantaneous opening, Origami spun around and escaped Ellen's restraint. She put power in the tip of her right foot and stretched her leg toward the other Wizard. A knife with a blade about ten centimeters long poked its face out. She coated the blade in magic and swung her leg.

"Hah! Ngh?!"

She felt an unmistakable impact with her foot, and Ellen groaned.

But then an invisible hand grabbed her foot and flung her at a building.

"...!"

Unable to decelerate in time, she slammed into the wall. She managed to absorb some of the impact, but the blow still knocked the wind out of her.

"Cough! Cough!"

"Well, you're something, hm?"

Still standing after the blast of mysterious magic, Ellen turned her gaze on Origami, her brow furrowed in irritation.

Her wiring suit was ripped from her chest down to her waist, and painful-looking tracks had been gouged into her pale skin. She had stopped the bleeding with her Territory, but traces of the blood that had scattered when she was injured stained her platinum armor red.

Ellen turned the tip of her sword on Origami.

"Albeit with some excessive outside assistance, you are the second person in my entire life to have injured my person, Origami Tobiichi. You are a magnificent Wizard. You should be confident and proud. But in the afterlife. Not in this world."

"Ngh..." Origami floated in the air, her aching body supported by her Territory. Although she'd managed to strike a blow, the already hopeless gap between her and Ellen had only opened up even farther.

But then Ellen's eyebrows twitched up and her gaze shifted, as though she was listening to something.

"Ike."

She glared at Origami again before turning her face toward Building 1.

"...! Where are you—," Origami said.

"It appears that's all the time we have," Ellen interrupted. "You're lucky."

"I-I won't let you!"

Shido was inside that building. Origami gave orders in her mind to go after Ellen.

However.

"Origami!"

She heard her name suddenly and began to glide swiftly through the air, her body wrapped in someone else's Territory.

A blast of cold air shot through the spot where she had been floating only a heartbeat earlier. If she had still been there, she would have been frozen solid along with her Territory.

"Ngh?!"

"You... What are you doing here?! You're supposed to be on strict bed rest!" The owner of the Territory that saved Origami looked down at her. A woman clad in a familiar wiring suit. AST Captain Ryouko Kusakabe.

"Captain?" Origami murmured.

"Yup. And what is with this equipment?" Ryouko frowned. "Is it SSS?"

"Let me go. I have to go after her—"

An incredible onslaught of wind and ice interrupted her. Ryouko furrowed her brow ever so slightly and manipulated the Territory that held Origami to evade the attack.

"Miss Miku's orders are...absolute...!"

"Keh-keh, so you flee then? But that only gives worth to the chase! I do so never tire of you humans!"

"Admiration. Master Origami is here. This is a battleground. Please leave immediately. In the event that you do not obey this instruction...I will dispose of even you, Master Origami."

A girl clinging to an enormous rabbit and two others with a wing each growing out of their backs danced in the air, and Origami gasped. The Spirit Hermit. And the students from the class next to Origami's, the Yamais.

"Kaguya, Yuzuru. You can't be...Spirits?" she asked, stunned.

But the Spirits themselves apparently could not have cared less about Origami's shock. The Yamai sisters cloaked their lance and pendulum in the currents of a roaring hurricane and then lobbed a mass of wind at Origami and Ryouko.

"Ngh—"

Origami broke away from Ryouko's Territory, fired her thrusters, and managed to escape further injury.

"Kah-kah! How well you perform!"

"Affirmation. But if you are hostile to Miss Miku, then we will show no mercy."

The Yamai sisters glared at her.

Discovering her throat suddenly very dry, Origami gulped and faced the Spirits alongside Ryouko.

Use the ID; open the door.

Shido looked around cautiously and then stepped into the room.

The walls were of a construction similar to the isolation area on *Fraxinus*, with a space surrounded by reinforced glass in the dimly lit research area.

"…!"

His eyes flew open. Tohka was inside the glass partition.

Perhaps she was sleeping—her head hung where she was restrained in a chair.

"Tohka!" he cried, but his voice didn't reach the other side of the reinforced glass.

Most likely, it was the same configuration as the space on *Fraxinus*. In which case, there had to be some control on this side that would allow him to get inside to Tohka. He sent his eyes racing around the room.

And then he froze in place.

He'd thought he and Miku were alone in the lab, but now he spotted a man sitting in a chair with his back turned to them.

"Ngh—"

Shido sharpened his gaze, fully on guard, and turned Sandalphon toward the man. Miku readied Gabriel's silver pipe.

"Aah, I've been waiting for you. You're Princess's…friend, I suppose?" the man said quietly and stood up. And then he turned slowly toward Shido and Miku. "I believe this is the first time we've met, yes? I'm Isaac Westcott of DEM Industries."

Dark ash blond hair, tall. Sharp eyes somehow reminiscent of a predator.

Looking at this face, hearing this name, Shido furrowed his brow minutely. "Isaac…Westcott."

Yes, this was the managing director of DEM Industries, Isaac Westcott. Anyone who had watched TV, read a newspaper, or checked out the news online would have heard his name at least once.

Westcott nodded rather dramatically. "How good of you to come. And Diva—" He looked at Miku, then turned his eyes back on Shido and cut himself off.

He looked befuddled for a moment and then frowned dubiously. "What…are you? You can't be… No, there's no way…" Westcott put a hand to his mouth as if considering something.

Not understanding what the man was up to, Shido frowned.

"I'm Shido Itsuka. I came to rescue Tohka! Set her free right now!" He turned the tip of Sandalphon toward Westcott.

Westcott's eyes opened wide. But not because he was shocked or frightened by having the Angel turned on him. He stared baffled at Shido for a moment.

"Shido...Itsuka. Hm?" he said finally. "Heh-heh! The boy who can use Spirit powers... I thought it was impossible when I first heard about you, but well now, I see. That's how it is. Heh-heh. Ha-ha! Ha-ha-ha-ha-ha-ha-ha-ha-ha!"

Shido grew even warier at this sudden change and tightened his grip on the Angel's hilt.

But Westcott paid him no mind as he laughed out loud, holding his stomach.

"Well, isn't this amusing? So in the end, everything is in the palm of *her* hand."

"What is going ooooon with this person?" Miku asked in a disgusted tone. "Does he have a few screws loose or something? Aah, this is why I haaaate men!"

"I don't think the fact that he's a man has anything to do with it," Shido replied, a little fed up, and then turned back to Westcott. "Laugh all you want. I don't care. Release Tohka!"

He thrust Sandalphon forward, and Westcott's shoulders shook merrily.

"And what will you do if I don't do as you ask?" the older man asked.

"Sorry, but you'll do it even if I have to force you to."

Westcott snickered. "I wonder if you could."

"I think I can," Shido told him. "I'd do anything to save Tohka."

"That was a joke." Westcott shrugged. "I'm not strong like Ellen. Up against a Spirit and a boy wielding an Angel, well, it's terrifying. Nothing I can do."

He began to tap at the nearby console.

Shido heard the sound of a quiet motor humming, and the area abruptly grew brighter. The shackles binding Tohka's wrists and ankles dropped away with a loud clatter.

"Tohka!" he shouted.

And his voice apparently could reach the other side of the glass now. He saw Tohka yank her head up where she was seated in the chair.

"*Shi...do...?*"

She sat up and rubbed her eyes like she was pushing away the sleep before looking in his direction.

"*Shido!*"

She finally realized that she hadn't been dreaming his voice. She leaped to her feet and ran toward him, ripping off the electrodes plastered to various parts of her body.

She pressed her palms and her forehead against the reinforced glass, looking like she was about to cry.

"*Shido...Shido. Shido!*"

"Hey... Sorry to keep you waiting, Tohka," he said, and she shook her head vigorously. The corners of his mouth slackened unconsciously.

She seemed to be okay. But it wasn't like he'd accomplished his goal yet. Although they could see and hear each other now, they were still separated by a thick sheet of glass.

"Hey, you," he snapped at Westcott. "Open the door."

"And release such a magnificent catch? Why don't you tear it open yourself?" Westcott said, shrugging.

Shido frowned in irritation. "Miku, do you mind?"

"Hmph!" She sniffed. "I do not appreciate being given directions by you, but this maaan is the person in charge here, yes? In that case, I will make an exception just this once. I was planning to let him heeeear my voice sooner or later anyway."

Miku took a step forward. A person could act as tough as they wanted to, but once they heard her voice, they would do whatever she wanted them to. It wouldn't be any trouble to get him to take this wall down.

But whether or not Westcott knew about Miku's abilities, he merely smiled, looking entirely at his ease.

"Ohh, yes, right. I forgot one thing, Shido Itsuka," he said quietly. "It's dangerous to stand there."

"Huh?" Shido replied. He had no idea what Westcott meant.

"Sh-Shido! *Behind you!*" Tohka cried out through the glass.

Zupp! Shido heard a curious sound, and felt something hot blooming in his chest.

"What?" he said, confused. He slowly lowered his gaze and finally realized that there was a laser blade thrusting out of his chest. "Wh— Th. This..."

Blood gushed from his mouth.

He shakily turned around to look behind him and saw a Wizard in a platinum CR unit.

"Ell...en...!"

"I will break any sword that points at Ike," Ellen said, impossibly dispassionate given the fact that she had just mortally wounded another human being. She pulled the blade of light out of Shido's chest with a similar lack of emotion.

"Ah. Gah..."

Shido was suddenly very unsteady on his feet. He leaned up against the glass wall. And then slid to the floor, leaving a trail of blood.

"*Shido! Shidoooooo!*"

Bang! Bang! He felt the vibrations. Tohka must have been beating her fists against the glass wall. But he was having trouble responding to her. The pain didn't leave much room for anything else in his mind, and he couldn't get his body to do what he wanted.

"Oh dear. It's not like you to be injured, isn't it?"

"I was careless. The Ratatoskr airship is likely in the air."

"Oh-ho?"

Shido heard Westcott and Ellen talking, but they sounded far away.

"He had an Angel manifested, so I attacked. Was that acceptable?"

"Yes. Fine. In fact, this way might be even better."

Westcott glanced at Tohka banging on the glass.

Kotori's blessing—the healing flames that bandaged up the injuries his body sustained—should still have been lodged in his body. And in fact, small flames were already lapping at the wound in his chest.

But perhaps because he was inside Ellen's Territory, or maybe because her blade had gone through his heart, or maybe even because he had forcibly used this blessing far too many times in a row today, the healing was more sluggish than usual. If he took another hit to the head or chest from the laser blade, Shido would be past the limits of healing and cross over onto the path to the afterlife.

"Toh. Ka."

He reached out for her, but blocked by the wall of glass, his hand dropped to the floor, leaving only a smear of blood.

"Ah."

Tohka stared, stunned, at the sight unfolding before her.

After coming to rescue her, Shido was now laying in a heap on the floor. After he had been stabbed through the chest, there was so much blood on the glass wall. He wasn't moving at all.

"Ah. Ah. Ah..." Tohka felt darkness descend over her world.

She had experienced this sensation just once before.

About five months earlier. The day of her first date with Shido. She had felt this exact way when Shido had been struck by Origami's evil weapon while protecting Tohka, and all the color disappeared from Tohka's emotions.

"Shido... Shido... Shido...!" She kept screaming his name as she slammed her fists against the glass.

She screamed, holding tightly on to her consciousness so that she wouldn't lose sight of herself. She knew Shido had Kotori's healing ability. That was why he had survived that time with Origami, and he would certainly be okay this time, too. The flames would lick at his wound, and he would smile at her again.

But. As if to squelch this hope of hers, Westcott turned his eyes toward her.

"Now then, Spirit. Princess. Tohka Yatogami. All the players are finally lined up. I am going to kill your precious Shido Itsuka."

"Wha—!" She gasped.

"Feel free to stop it if you can. I won't interfere. Use everything you have to stop Ellen's blade. Your Astral Dress, your Angel. And if those aren't enough, reach your hand out even further."

"What...are you talking about..."

"You'll understand soon enough. Ellen." Westcott raised a hand, and Ellen Mathers slowly moved to stand beside Shido.

"Are you certain, Ike?"

"Yes. While I am indeed curious about Shido Itsuka, our priority is Princess. If, in the worst case, she dies, the Sefirah won't shatter. So either way is fine."

"*I see,*" Ellen said, and raised the laser blade in her hands.

"_____!"

Miku raised her lovely voice from where she stood farther back in the room, but Ellen only twitched an eyebrow.

Westcott, too, had a cool look on his face, protected as he was by Ellen's Territory. *"It's pointless, Diva. You can't seduce me with just that."*

"Wha...!" Confusion colored Miku's face.

Ellen took her eyes off Miku and looked down at Shido as she tightened her grip on the laser blade.

"Wh-what are you doing?" Tohka asked, unable to understand what Ellen was attempting.

Actually, she did understand. She understood, but her head refused to accept it.

After all, if that blade came down, Shido would really die.

Shido would.

Shido, who had given her such a happy life.

Shido, who had shown Tohka the beauty of the world when she was sunk into the deepest despair.

He wouldn't move anymore.

He wouldn't talk to her anymore.

He wouldn't smile at her anymore.

"Ah! Aaaaaaaaah!"

The moment she accepted this reality, Tohka stomped on the ground.

"Sandalphon! Sandalphon!" she shouted, stomping on the floor and beating the glass so hard, her hands were nearly bleeding.

Her body shone faintly, and a dress of light materialized around her school uniform.

An Astral Dress. One of the elements that made a Spirit a Spirit, a most powerful suit of armor. This was followed by the Angel Sandalphon forming in Tohka's right hand.

But for some reason, its magnificent light was not enough this time. No matter how she sliced at the invisible wall that separated her from Shido, she couldn't cut through it.

"Why... Why? Why!"

She brought her sword down against the wall over and over. But to no avail.

Ellen added her left hand to the hilt of the laser blade she held in her right.

"Stop! Stop! Stop it! Just this. Just Shido!" she begged. "I don't care what happens to me! I'll do anything! I'll do whatever you want! So... So please don't take Shido from me!"

But Ellen was not interested in hearing her pleas. The muscles in her arms tensed.

Tohka swung Sandalphon and hacked at the wall with a force that threatened to break her arms. But she didn't so much as scratch the glass. She clearly needed more power.

Her Angel was not enough.

"Stoooooooooooooooooooooooooooop!"

She'd take anything. She howled like a wild animal, tears staining her face. She didn't care if it wasn't the Angel anymore. If it would get them out of this. If she could just save Shido, she didn't care what the power was or where it came from. If she could cut through this wall and beat Ellen back, she didn't care what happened to her!

The blade of shining light was brought down toward Shido's neck.

"Aaaaaaaaaaaaaaaaaaaaaaaaaaaaaaaaaaaaaaaaaaaaaaaaaaaaaaaaa aaaaaaaaaaaaaaaaaaaaaaaaaaaaaaaaaaaaaaaaaaaaaaaaaaaaaaaaaaa aaaaaaaaaaaaaaaaaaaaaaaaaaaaaaaaaaaaaaaaaaaaaaaaaaaaaaaaaaa aaaaaaaaaaaaaaaaaaaaaaaaaaaaaaaaaaaaaaaaaaaaaah!"

At the same time as her consciousness mind snapped, Tohka felt like she was holding something other than her Angel in her right hand.

No. Perhaps this was...

It was maybe more like she was being *made* to hold something.

A shrill alarm squealed on the bridge of *Fraxinus*.

Kotori's eyebrows jumped up.

This alarm was generally never used. It was a herald of the direst state of emergency.

"What?!" she cried, looking at the monitor.

But Mana was still engaged in battle with the massive unit, and Kotori couldn't see any anomalies on any of the other screens. At the very least, she couldn't see anything that would make this alarm go off.

She frowned dubiously and then heard Shiizaki cry out from in front of her console.

"Eep!"

"What is it?" Kotori demanded.

"I-it's..." Shiizaki turned her gaze toward Kotori, her fingers shaking slightly. "C-Commander... *Fraxinus*'s measurement devices are still not back to normal...or something, right?"

"Uhhh? What are you talking about?" Kotori said. "It's mainly the communications stuff that got all messed up. Now answer me. What exactly has happened?"

Shiizaki swallowed hard before opening her mouth again. "C-Category E... The Spirit value is showing a negative...?!"

"Wha—" Kotori's eyes flew open.

And then, with perfect timing, an anomaly appeared on the external feed displayed on the submonitor.

The top floor of the building Shido was in began to glow with a dark energy that radiated outward toward the sky.

"Impossible."

The worst thing imaginable was happening. The thing she had feared had become reality.

"Sefirah...inversion!" Kotori groaned, and bit down on her Chupa Chups.

"Ha-ha-ha-ha! Ha-ha-ha-ha-ha-ha-ha-ha-ha-ha!"

The instant Ellen moved to bring her sword down on the neck of Shido Itsuka, Westcott burst into laughter.

The body of Princess, Tohka Yatogami, had abruptly turned black. She emitted a vivid darkness, and then an indiscernible mix of light and dark particles spilled out of her and melted the reinforced glass as if it were made of butter. The stream shot through the walls and the windows, and dispersed in all directions.

"Ike, this is—," Ellen asked, stunned, her hand stopped in her great surprise.

Westcott put the flood of emotion in his heart into his voice as he murmured, "The kingdom has inverted. Now, brace yourselves, humanity."

He spread out his hands.

"This is the triumphant return of the demon king."

Chapter 10
Slaughter, Tyrant

"Ah-ha-ha-ha-ha-ha-ha-ha-ha-ha-ha-ha-ha-ha-ha-ha-ha! Die die die die die die die die die die die die die die die die dieeeeeeeeeee!"

Hundreds of missiles and bullets accompanied this deranged laughter, scattering through the air.

Mana increased the strength of her Territory and managed to defend against this concentrated onslaught.

But, as if aiming for this very opening, Jessica deployed a limited Territory around her.

"Tch!" Mana clicked her tongue in vexation, twisted her body, and sliced through the Territory with the laser edge in her right hand, Wolftail.

But by the time she did this, Jessica had already finished recharging her magic guns. She turned the massive weapon Blast Arc on Mana and fired.

"Should have been more careful!"

Mana contracted her Territory, and the stream of magic slid past above her. She charged at Jessica, swinging Wolftail.

Naturally, Jessica also went on the defensive with her Territory and deftly guarded against Mana's attack.

Mana's blade slammed into a magic wall, sending showers of sparks flying.

But here a change appeared in Jessica.

"H...?!" She convulsed, and blood poured from her eyes and nose while the Territory that enveloped her abruptly grew weaker.

Jessica's flagging Territory couldn't withstand Mana's laser edge. The blade cut into the red mechanical body of Licorice and annihilated the laser blade and magic gun in Jessica's left hand.

But Jessica leaped back, and Mana grimaced. "You're at your activation limit, Jessica! This fight's already over! Accept—"

Jessica ignored Mana and turned her remaining gun on her. And then fired a shot that was unbelievable, given that she was up against her activation limit.

"Hngh…" Mana dodged the blast at the last second and turned sharp eyes on the other girl.

Jessica grinned maniacally, tears of blood streaming down her face.

"Mana. Mana. Mana Takamiya. No. N-n-n-no more, no more los-s-s-s-s-sing. I'm not losing. I won't lose. As long as I have Licorice, I-I-I h-h-ha-ha-ha-ha-ha-ha-ha-ha-ha-ha-ha-ha!" Unfocused eyes swimming, Jessica stammered like a skipping record. She was clearly not in a normal state of mind.

"Jessica…" Mana bit her lip and clenched her hands so tightly, she almost drew blood.

She didn't know exactly what, but some kind of magical processing had definitely been carried out on Jessica's brain. Something that took the decades of life ahead of her and compressed them all into this one day. That explained why she was strong.

Mana stared at her with eyes filled with anguish and pity as she sighed quietly. And then without a word, she put a hand to her chest.

She had already been told by Kotori and Reine that something similar had been done to her own body. If she had made even one misstep, she might have ended up like Jessica.

"…"

Silently, Mana gritted her teeth.

"Manaaa! M-M-M-Mana. Mana Takamiya. Adeptus Number Twooooo. I never liked you, you know. Why. Wh-wh-wh-wh-wh-why would Mr. Westcott and L-Leader M-M-Mathers appoint an Easterner like you-you-you-you-you? I. I-I'm…much better. For the job. For A. A-A-A-A-A-A-Adeptus Number Two!"

Still rambling, Jessica fired her weapon wildly.

But rather than evading these shots, Mana deployed her defensive Territory and slowly approached the other Wizard.

"It's always been like this with you. You're so jealous and ambitious, and yet every word out of your mouth is a mess," she said softly as she closed the distance between them.

Even after Mana was quite close, Jessica didn't move to pull away, but continued to fire recklessly.

"But your loyalty is worthy of respect," Mana continued. "I loathed you, but this should never have been done to you."

"Ha! Ah-ha-ha-ha-ha-ha-ha-ha! Maaaaaaaaaanaaaaaaa?" Jessica looked at Mana with unfocused eyes as she opened her weapons container and launched a barrage of micro missiles.

Mana advanced through this rain of artillery, made the laser edge in her right arm vibrate, and sliced through Jessica's chest.

"Ah. Gah. Ah. Aaaaaah!"

She felt it rip through her Territory, through her wiring suit, into her human skin. But Mana didn't avert her eyes.

The Territory around Jessica disappeared, and the massive mechanical body of Scarlet Licorice dropped toward the earth.

Jessica, supported by Mana's Territory, spoke weakly as she bled out. "Heeey. Hey hey hey. Heeey. Manaaaa? I-I-I-I. I'm strong, riiight? No one's ever gonna beat me again. Y-you think Mr. Westcott will r-r-r-r-recognize thaaat?"

"...Yes, of course he will," Mana said, and Jessica smiled.

And then her head slumped forward.

"..."

Mana closed Jessica's eyes, pulled her body close to her, and glared in the direction of DEM Building 1.

"Isaac...Westcott!"

"...!"

Shido was lying in a pool of his own blood, flames licking at his wound as he stared at the scene unfolding before him.

The instant that Ellen moved to thrust her sword of light at him, Tohka shrieked loud enough to rip her throat wide open, and then, her body was enveloped by particles of black light.

"What...is..."

The flames were finally blocking the wound in his chest. Fighting the sense of nausea that rose up in his throat, he somehow managed to move a mouth filled with the taste of iron.

Something was clearly off.

Behind him, Westcott raised his voice in excitement, but Shido couldn't catch a word of what he was saying. Actually, to be more precise, he could hear the sounds of the words, but his brain failed to process their meaning.

That's how fixed his eyes were to the abnormal phenomenon happening to Tohka.

But that was no wonder. Whatever this was, it was very obviously different from the times before when Tohka had summoned limited versions of her Astral Dress and Angel.

An ominous black light radiated outward from her darkened silhouette, and he was finally able to catch a glimpse of Tohka herself.

"Wha..." He took one look at her and gasped.

The Tohka that emerged from inside the black light was clad in an Astral Dress. Which wasn't outrageous in and of itself. Although Shido had sealed her power inside him, there was something like an invisible path between him and the Spirits. When a Spirit's emotions reached an extreme, part of her Spirit power would flow back through that channel.

This didn't happen only with Tohka. Yoshino and the Yamai sisters had also gone against the will of Ratatoskr from time to time and manifested their Astral Dress or Angels.

But what hung on Tohka's body now was clearly not a limited Astral Dress. Shining, jet-black armor on her shoulders and hips. And a veil the color of darkness with no material form spread out to cover her chest and lower half. This was an Astral Dress in a complete state, woven with concentrated Spirit power.

"Astral. Dress..."

But the one Tohka was wearing now was a different shape and color from the one in Shido's memory. It was like he was looking at the negative of a photo.

And there was something even more concerning. The expression on her face.

This was not the Tohka of a few seconds earlier, weeping and screaming his name. This was the face of a king, radiating an air of aloof intimidation.

Naturally, it wasn't as though the structure of her face or body had changed. And yet, for some reason, Shido couldn't help but feel that the girl who had stepped forth from inside the black light was an entirely separate creature from Tohka.

"That's…" Shido lifted his wobbly head.

Tohka, clad in this black Astral Dress, held a remarkably massive sword in her right hand.

"Sandal…phon?"

No. It wasn't. This was clearly a different sword.

Enormous and single-edged. Hilt and scabbard colored with the same darkness as her Astral Dress, and the blade left an arc of hazy black light in space.

"—!"

A shiver ran up his spine, and he swallowed hard. For some reason, there was something about this sword that frightened him and made him shiver unconsciously, something other than the blade or its threat as a weapon, or the great Spirit power it held.

"…"

With a composed demeanor, Tohka looked around. And then she let out a short sigh. "What is this place?"

"Huh?" Shido frowned. What was she talking about?

Seeming not to notice his question, Tohka sent her eyes around the room and pointed at Miku. "You. Answer me. Where am I?"

"What? Umm, isn't this…DEM Industries Japan braaanch?"

"Never heard of it. So then why am I here?"

"Oh, didn't that Wizard there abduct you?" Miku turned toward Ellen and Westcott, looking perplexed.

Following her gaze, Tohka turned her eyes in their direction.

A broad grin spread across Westcott's face. "Magnificent. I've never seen such a wonderful inversion. Look, Ellen. *That* is our dream. Our heartfelt desire."

He clasped Ellen's shoulder.

"Now, time to go to work. An opponent worthy of you has at last come to stand before you. My most powerful Wizard. Take the head of this treacherous demon king and make it the cornerstone of our plan."

"Yes, I understand, Ike." Ellen had no sooner nodded than she vanished like mist.

In the next instant, she appeared above Tohka's head and swung the laser blade in her hand.

"…!"

On his hands and knees, Shido tried to warn Tohka. But it was too sudden. He couldn't get a shout out.

It seemed his concern was unnecessary, however. Without turning her face, Tohka threw her right hand up and blocked Ellen's attack with her sword. The moment their blades touched, a powerful shockwave shot outward, and Shido was thrown into the wall.

"Ngh…!"

The impact raced through his not-yet-healed wound, and Shido grimaced and let out a groan.

Miku ran over to him. "Hey? Are you okaaay?!"

It was not like Miku to worry about a boy. Maybe she was shaken up by all this, too.

That made sense. Shido also had no idea what was going on. If someone had told him that this was a vision he was having as he lay on death's doorstep, he would have accepted that explanation without question.

"Impudent," Tohka murmured, having stopped the laser blade attack and sent Ellen flying.

Ellen whirled herself around and froze in midair. "It seems that you *are* different from the princess we've seen so far. I suppose it would be an issue if you weren't. A Spirit I can easily defeat would be meaningless."

"What are you?" Tohka asked. "Why do you swing your sword at me?"

"My sincerest apologies, but I need you to die now. All we require is your strength. Your personality is nothing but a hindrance," Ellen said, sharpening her gaze. She brandished her laser blade once more and leaped at Tohka.

Tohka added her left hand to the hilt of the sword and swept the blade outward to stop Ellen's attack.

But Ellen did not stop her fierce charge. She swung her sword so fast that it left only afterimages from the side, from above, from below.

Shido forgot to even cry out as he stared at the glittering afterimage of the laser blade that shone in his field of vision. The speed and drive were obviously different from the Ellen he'd seen so far. She attacked multiple times in an instant with a ferocity that likely would have cut Tohka down on the first blow if she had still been in her limited unlocked state.

Tohka, however, did not pale in comparison to this. She caught each and every one of the blows with a swordsmanship that would have been impossible for a human being, dispatching them all handily.

A fight beyond human knowledge between someone who was not human and someone who exceeded human abilities. Even though none of the attacks were turned on him, he felt like he might be crushed by the fierce bloodlust and hostility hanging in the air around the fighters.

"There!"

From a lowered position, Ellen lifted her sword against Tohka's and knocked Tohka's blade upward. Instantly, Tohka was wide open.

"Mm…"

Of course, Ellen was the same, with her sword raised high. But when she nimbly drew herself back, the weapon on the left side of her back shifted and reached forward from her side. At the same time, a light converged on its tip.

"Pierce, Rhongomyniad."

Instantly, a dazzling flash of light emitted from the weapon.

The magical light was so concentrated, it threatened to burn out the eyes of anyone looking at it directly. The weapons used by the AST didn't even begin to compare. This was an overwhelming destructive power that rivaled a blow from an Angel.

Tohka was swallowed up by magic, and the walls and ceiling of the building were blown away as if they had been made out of paper. Even this could not quench the power of the light—aftershocks rippled up out into the sky.

The attack was slightly different in nature from a simple bombardment. If Shido had to describe it—yes, it was a lance.

A massive lance of light, hundreds of meters long, butchered everything in its path to stand tall in the air.

A heartbeat later, Ellen let out a shallow breath and the enormous lance vanished. The walls and ceiling were gouged away along with the upper floors, making the building look almost as if a giant had taken a bite out of it.

"Tohka... Tohka?!" Shido called and looked around, but he couldn't see any sign of her.

What if the attack had blown her away without a trace... This disturbing image flitted through the back of his mind.

But that thought dissipated the moment he caught sight of Ellen's face as she glared at the sky, showing no sign of letting her guard down.

They had a much better view of the sky now. Against the backdrop of the moon, Tohka was calmly looking down at them, shining skirt fluttering. She had most likely guarded against the attack with her sword. He couldn't see so much as a scratch on her.

"I see. So you're not all talk." Tohka narrowed her eyes and slowly raised the sword in her right hand.

"I won't allow it." Ellen didn't just sit back and watch Tohka. The moment she readied her laser blade again, she lunged for Tohka with a slash at her chest.

"Hmph." Tohka scowled ever so slightly, and caught the blow not with her sword, but with her empty left hand.

But even Tohka's Astral Dress couldn't completely stop Ellen's attack. Waves of intense magic sparked and scattered, the long glove on Tohka's hand ripped, and wounds that looked like fine burn lines spidered up her arm.

However.

"Nahemah," Tohka said in a cool voice, ignoring the burning of her own left hand. She held the sword—Nahemah—up high against the moon and then brought it downward.

Not toward Ellen.

Toward Isaac Westcott.

"Ngh!" Ellen scowled for the first time, immediately ceased her attack on Tohka, fired her thrusters, and raced to the building.

Whssh! A roar cut through the turbulent air, and then space itself creaked and groaned.

An instant later, an immense shock wave shot out from the tip of Tohka's sword.

"Unh. Waaaaah?!"

"Eeeeeeeeek!"

Shido and Miku screamed as this blast wave reached them.

Miku's scream, however, appeared to contain Spirit power. An invisible wall grew up around them and softened the blow of the blast shaking the space around them.

"A-are you okay, Miku?!" he asked.

"Y-yes… Also, just so you know, I didn't intend to saaave you just now! It was merely coincidence!" Miku turned her face away, a look of utmost reluctance on it.

But if it hadn't been for Miku's wall of sound, Shido would probably have been sent flying through the air from just the lingering after-effects of the blast wave.

He looked at the deep crevices carved out of the floor and blanched.

"Tohka? Is that…you?" His face was colored with fear as he looked up at the black silhouette hanging in the sky.

Clatter. He heard something crumbling, and then Ellen and Westcott appeared from behind a heap of rubble. It seemed that before Tohka's blow could erase Westcott, Ellen had stopped it with her Territory.

"Sorry," Westcott said. "Thanks for that, Ellen."

"Not at all. I can't allow you to die now," Ellen replied, her eyes still on Tohka.

"So? How is this Princess then?"

"The last time I fought her doesn't begin to compare. That was somewhat of a let-down, but now I can see why she has the AAA rank."

"Oh-ho." Westcott whistled, impressed. "Well, you can beat her, yes?"

"Of course. There isn't a creature on this earth who can defeat me," she replied without a hint of hesitation. And then paused before continuing. "When I am in top condition, that is."

Shido lowered his eyes and gasped.

Blood was pouring from the deep wound that ran from Ellen's collar down to her waist.

"My attention was taken up with defense, and the wound I sustained earlier opened up," she said. "I have implemented pain management, but I'm somewhat at a disadvantage against that Spirit."

"Mm-hmm. I see." Westcott put a hand to his chin and sighed. "Well, if that's how it is, we'll withdraw now. We still have time. We'll get this done right."

"Are you certain?"

"Mm-hmm. I'm used to waiting. The fact that we were able to invert Princess at all is a great success. And I was also able to meet an unexpected face today." Westcott turned his gaze on Shido, and Shido jumped. "Terribly sorry, but we will have to excuse ourselves here. If you survive, let's meet again. Shido Takamiya—I mean, Itsuka."

"Huh?" Shido frowned.

Takamiya. That was the surname of Mana, who proclaimed herself to be his little sister.

"Hang on a second," he said. "What do you know about me?!"

"Nothing at all. Not about Shido Itsuka." Westcott turned his eyes away from Shido and put a hand on Ellen's shoulder.

In the next instant, the air around Ellen distorted. She had likely contracted the Territory deployed around her. She floated Westcott up into the air, as if supporting him with an invisible hand, fired her thrusters, and shot off into the distant sky.

"Ah! H-hey!" Shido shouted, but they had already disappeared into the dark night. His voice simply echoed in vain.

Although the enemy was now gone, the situation hadn't yet been resolved.

Tohka chased after the disappearing Ellen and Westcott with her eyes before looking down and catching sight of Shido and Miku. She slowly descended toward them.

"All that's left is you two then?" she said, looking at them with cold eyes.

Shido tensed up at this look, impossible from the usual Tohka.

"Hey. Aren't you supposed to knooooow each other? Also, this girl's super strong. Like, she didn't need you to come rescue her. What on eaaarth is going on?" Miku asked in a small voice.

But Shido had no answer for her. "I mean...I don't know what's going on here, either."

"Also, you got stabbed riiiight in the chest, right? How are you still alive?"

"That's... Well, let's call it my special feature. I'll explain later," he told her, and then turned his attention back to Tohka. He couldn't exactly face off against her without saying anything at all, so he started to open his mouth.

But Tohka casually swung Nahemah, producing an impact wave that shot straight at Shido and Miku.

"Whoa?!"

"Eeek!"

He unconsciously intercepted the blow with Sandalphon. He managed to stay on his feet somehow, but the hands that gripped the hilt shrieked in pain.

"Ngh!" He shuddered. Maybe it was just child's play for Tohka, but that blow had definitely been aimed squarely at him. The slicing attack was such that if he hadn't stopped it with Sandalphon, he might have been killed.

"So it *is* Sandalphon," Tohka said, her eyes narrowing sharply. The look on her face was clearly hostile. "Why do you have that Angel?"

"Tohka! You... What's wrong with you?! Don't you remember me?!" Shido shouted.

Tohka frowned. "Tohka? Me?"

She stared hard at his face. This was indeed not the usual Tohka. Not only did she not remember Shido, she didn't even remember her own name.

"What...on earth..." Shido furrowed his brow in confusion.

Abruptly, he heard a burst of static from the earpiece in his right ear, followed by Kotori's voice. It seemed that whatever had been jamming the signal had disappeared with the destruction of the upper part of the building.

"Shido! Shido! Respond! What happened?!"

"Dunno!" he cried. "Tohka got weird when Ellen stabbed me! Is this her Spirit power flowing back into her?!"

"No. Probably not."

"So then what? Can I seal the Spirit power of this Tohka, too?!"

"That...I don't know. There's no precedent. But more importantly, with her likability for you low right now, there's no way."

"So then what am I supposed to do?!"

"You'll just have to bring Tohka's mind back somehow. If there is a possibility, then it's..."

Kotori went over this "possibility." Shido's eyebrows jumped up.

"Makes sense. So then what I do is still the same?"

"What are you mumbling about?" Tohka asked in an icy voice, interrupting the conversation between Shido and Kotori. "Hmph. I don't know what it is, but I don't care. If I slaughter you, it'll be over. And you don't seem to have as much power as that woman before."

Tohka swept her sword out once more. A shock wave assaulted Shido.

"Ngah!"

He managed to defend himself against the first blow somehow, but in the next instant, Tohka was swinging her blade again. The slicing attack came flying at Shido. His hands were numb. He couldn't raise his own sword to defend himself against the blast.

"Ngh—"

"Aaaaaaaaaaaaaaaaaaaaaaaaaaaaah!"

Miku shrieked, building an invisible wall to just barely save Shido from the shock wave.

"Miku!" he said.

"Please don't get the wrooong idea. I told you, didn't I? What I hate most of all is men who throw around words like *love* and *important* and *I would die for* and then change their minds at the drop of a hat."

"Huh?"

"You said you would save Tohka even if it meant your liiiife, didn't you?" Miku continued. "Please see that out to the end. Please...don't disappoint me. I...came here to see that."

"Miku..." Shido looked at her and then nodded firmly. "Right. Okay."

He readjusted his grip on Sandalphon and glared at Tohka.

"Okay, Tohka. It'll be morning soon. Let's go home and have breakfast. If you say sorry right now, I'll make all your favorites for you."

"What are you talking about?" Tohka frowned suspiciously.

Shido let out a long breath and then charged her.

Tohka swung her sword.

Shido managed to defend with Sandalphon, but he ended up pushed back to the very spot he'd started from.

"Hngh!"

"What are you dooooing? Very bad look."

"Shut up," Shido said. "There isn't any other way! I can't do anything unless I get close to her!"

Miku arched an eyebrow. "So you're saaaaying there's a way to save her if you can get close to her?"

"Yeah." He nodded. "As to whether it'll work or not, I won't know unless I try."

"Hmm. I see," Miku replied indifferently, and then whirled around and hit the ground with the soles of her feet, as if she were tap dancing. "Gabriel. Rondo."

Several silver pipes rose up from the ground to surround Miku, the ends pointed toward her like microphones.

No, that wasn't all. The metal pipes of a pipe organ appeared all over what was left of the floor of the building, and the tips of those shifted toward Tohka.

"Fine," Miku said. "Just this once. I will give you a chance, you endlessly foolish, simple-minded boy who came this far all by yourself for Tohka's sake."

"Huh?"

"I will slam Tohka from all directions with a defensive voice. I don't know how many seconds it will last against her, but it should be able to stop her from moving for a little bit. During that time, please go tryyyy whatever this way of yours is."

"Miku, you..."

"Will you do it? Or no?" Miku asked in a tone that brooked no reproach.

Shido looked at Tohka, braced his feet, and nodded firmly. "You bet!"

"Then here we go."

Miku threw her head back and took a deep breath.

"————————————!"

She aimed the high-pitched voice that reverberated in his ears toward the silver pipes of her Angel standing all around her.

Gabriel's silver conduits amplified Miku's voice, pinning Tohka down with invisible hands. Her arms twisted unnaturally to press tightly against her body, as if they had been tied there with a rope.

"Mm. What...is this." Tohka scowled unhappily, and flexed her arms to try and break free. Each time she did, Miku's voice grew shriller, like she was in pain.

"Mi—"

Shido curbed the impulse to call out her name and kicked at the floor.

Nothing he could say to her in that moment meant anything. In fact, it would only be a waste of a second of the precious time she had bought for him.

In which case, Shido had to move forward. If he was really thinking of Miku, he had to reach Tohka as soon as possible. He had to bring her mind back. He didn't have a second to spare!

"Hmph..." Tohka had apparently noticed him approaching. She kicked at the floor with a foot, and the concrete shattered and flew at Shido like buckshot.

"Ngah!"

Although he blocked some of the fragments with Sandalphon, chunks of concrete slammed into various parts of his body. He nearly stopped his charge forward at the sudden intense pain that came over him.

But he couldn't exactly stop and stand there. Guarding his face with his hand, he gritted his teeth against the oncoming attack and the shrieking pain and charged toward Tohka.

Tohka clicked her tongue in annoyance. "What a bother." She took a deep breath, bent forward, and forced her arms outward, ripping apart the restraints of sound.

"—?!"

Miku's voice steadily grew hoarser.

"—"

Miku's eyes flew open in despair.

In order to resist and push back against Tohka's steadily increasing power, she had amplified the strength of the restraint. But then her voice abruptly gave out.

"—, —"

She tried to murmur "why," but no sound came out. There was just air whistling in her throat.

"Wha...!" Shido cried out in confusion.

"Hmph." Tohka grunted in annoyance.

At the same time as Miku's voice died out, Gabriel's silver pipes fell over with a *clank*, and the wall of sound restraining Tohka disappeared completely.

She had most likely consumed too much Spirit power. That day, she had been using her voice and her Angel nonstop, more than she ever had before. On top of that, she had even been reckless enough to use a defensive voice wall and restrain an overwhelmingly more powerful Spirit like Tohka. It was no wonder her Spirit power cut out and she could no longer speak.

"Hmph. How impertinent." Tohka snorted and brandished Nahemah.

Not at Shido, but at Miku.

"Wha...!" Shido gasped, but he still wasn't close enough to leap at Tohka.

"Thinking you could tie me up. Know your place," Tohka said and brought her sword down.

"—"

Miku tried to scream, but of course, nothing came out. She smiled lifelessly and, instead of trying to avoid the attack, sank down to the floor. More accurately, she didn't have the strength left to evade.

In a second, Nahemah would cut into her. Fortunately, her Astral Dress hadn't disappeared with her voice, although she doubted that it could hold up against a blow from that Angel.

There was nothing she could do about that.

Miku had only ever had her singing. She had never had anything else. So now that she had lost her song, her voice, her sound, Miku had no value.

Without her song, no one would love her. Without her voice, no one would protect her. Without her sound, no one would believe her.

She had known this very well for a long time.

Now that she thought about it, it only made sense that it would turn out like this. She had jumped into a building swarming with Wizards. The very fact that she had deliberately come to a place like this had been a mistake.

She finally had three of her long-desired Spirits under her control. She had been enjoying herself immensely, so why had she even come here?

Miku interrogated herself, and quickly smiled helplessly.

Right. That boy. Shido Itsuka.

She had come to see the boy who had said the insincere words Miku hated most of all, that he was going to save Tohka even if it meant giving up his own life. To see his resolve. Or his pathetic end.

She'd been surprised when she heard Shido Itsuka had shown up at DEM Industries. She hadn't expected he would actually expose himself to danger and go to rescue Tohka.

If she were being entirely honest, she wanted to see it herself, just once.

Miku had been pushed to despair because of human beings, because of this creature called a man.

That was why she wanted to see a human being who truly loved someone else from the bottom of their heart.

Shido hadn't given up, right until the end. He had literally spat blood and kept walking in order to take back this person who was so important to him. Even if it killed him.

What if.

What if she had met a boy like this sooner.

What if even a tiny bit of the love he had for Tohka had been turned toward her.

I could have gone down a different path…, she said in a soundless voice and lowered her eyes.

However.

"Mikuuuuuuuuu!"

Shido roared her name, and Miku's closed eyes flew open.

Shouting Miku's name, Shido changed course half-subconsciously.

It wasn't because of cold calculation that he could never reach Tohka at this distance. His body simply moved because he had to help Miku. That was all.

He couldn't let Miku die.

And he couldn't let Tohka kill Miku.

But this slicing attack now was different from the playful blows earlier. Shido probably wouldn't be able to defend against it completely with Sandalphon. He wouldn't be able to completely protect Miku with just the power he had now.

Something more. He needed one more thing.

If he had the power to protect Miku…!

The moment Shido made this wish…

"…?!"

…he felt a cold sensation in his left hand.

"Huh…?!" Yoshino cried out softly as she did battle with the AST Wizards, dancing through the air on Zadkiel's back.

She had condensed the water out of the air and formed it into icicles, and just as she was about to launch these at the Wizards, she was overcome by a strange sensation, as if a thin membrane set up around her own mind had been pulled away. Or as if a tree in her head had been yanked up by the roots.

"What was that... Huh? Huh?" A heartbeat later, she looked around with wide eyes.

What on earth was she doing?

Her head was filled with this fundamental question.

No, she did understand what she was doing. She had materialized her Astral Dress and her Angel Zadkiel and was fighting the AST.

But...why?

"Unh..." Her head throbbed when she had this thought.

Yoshinon inside Zadkiel also raised a curious voice.

"Huh? Yoshinoooo. What are we doing here?"

"Y-you, too, Yoshinon...?"

"Yeah. It's, like, there's a big hole in my head or something. I remember watching everyone onstage at the Tenou Festival... But. But. But."

Yoshinon started to stammer strangely and wriggled its enormous body around like it was itchy.

Yoshino opened her eyes wide at this sudden movement. "Wh-what's wrong, Yoshinon?"

"Mm, nah, it's just I felt this different weird thing from the other weird thing..."

"Weird...thing?"

"Yeah, yeah. I dunno. It almost feels like, maybe my power being sucked away?"

"...?" Yoshino cocked her head to one side curiously.

But they couldn't have a leisurely conversation about it. The reason was simple. Wary of Yoshino and Yoshinon after they suddenly stopped attacking, the members of the AST all began to fire their Gatling guns at them.

"Eep!"

"Wh-whoa!"

Yoshino held her breath, and Yoshinon glided through the air, avoiding the rain of bullets at the last second.

But of course, the attack didn't end there. Another group standing by to the rear turned laser cannons on them.

"Good! Fire!" a woman who appeared to be the captain cried out, and the Wizards pulled their triggers.

But a heartbeat faster than they were, a ferocious wind swirled down around the AST members.

"Ngah?!"

The absurd energy of it, a large-scale typhoon compressed into a few meters' space, tossed the AST members and their Territories in all directions. The magical light released from their laser cannons stretched out into the sky or down to the ground, where there was no one to hit.

"Kah-kah! Light! So very light! This is what it means to fly. Although, well, an attempt to defend against a blow of our Raphael would perhaps be a crueler tale!"

"Question. Are you injured? Yoshino? Yoshinon?"

The girls who brought about the wind flew lightly through the sky to Yoshino's side.

"Kaguya... Yuzuru!" Yoshino shouted, and the sisters clad in the same maid uniform as Yoshino nodded firmly in response.

But even after being hit with that compressed hurricane, one shadow still came to attack the Yamai sisters. A girl in a suit different from those of the other AST personnel—Origami. She brandished her laser claw and charged toward the twins.

"—!"

But Origami was already seriously battered. Kaguya blew a compressed mass of air at her, which hit her squarely in the stomach, and Origami doubled over.

Yuzuru gently held up Origami's body when it started to drop helplessly toward the ground. "Confusion. Master Origami. What on earth..."

"Shi...do..." Origami said this before losing consciousness completely.

Yuzuru looked perplexed. Gently cradling Origami, she glided over to the AST she had only just knocked flying, carefully handed Origami over to them, and then returned to Yoshino and Kaguya.

"Wh-what are you...," the captain who accepted Origami asked dubiously.

But Yoshino had no answer. She also would have liked to know what she was doing there.

"And yet a lone question lingers, Yoshino. Why are we in a place such as this?"

"Assent. I thought we were at the Tenou Festival."

It seemed that the Yamai sisters also did not have any kind of grasp on the situation. And Yoshino had been hoping they might be able to tell her something.

"...!"

Yoshino, the Yamai sisters, and Yoshinon inside Zadkiel yanked their heads upward, turning their eyes to the top floor of the largest building in the area.

It was a battlefield, chaotic with muffled roars and scattered beams of magical light. They watched the massive explosion and incredible surge of Spirit power.

"Wh-what...," Yoshino murmured, stunned, as she looked up at the explosion, and then met the eyes of the Yamai sisters, who looked similarly shocked.

"Ah."

Perhaps thanks to the brief rest, her voice had recovered somewhat. Miku managed to make a faint sound.

But even before that, before her precious voice, her mind was taken up with what was happening in front of her eyes.

Shido was standing between her and Tohka, defending her against the blow from Nahemah. His left hand was held out, creating a barrier of what could only be described as a wall of cold air.

"...?!"

The temperature around her dropped precipitously, and a white haze drifted past her. Perhaps from the aftereffects of the Spirit power, small crystals of moisture condensed out of the air, danced down, touched Miku's skin, and melted.

Miku had seen this before.

Yes. It was very similar to the power of Yoshino's Angel Zadkiel.

"Hey...Miku, you okay?" Shido said, and glanced down at her.

"Ut. Ah you—," she said, still unable to produce much of a voice or even sound coherent.

Holding back the blow from Nahemah, Shido opened his mouth as he made the wall of cold air disperse. "I promised you."

"Huh...?" Miku frowned, and then her shoulders jumped up as she gasped.

She remembered the conversation they'd had in the building earlier.

So then what? You're saying that if I was in trouble like Tohka is, you'd risk your life to save me or something?!

Of course! had indeed been Shido's response.

Miku put a hand to her mouth and shivered. Tears spilled from her wide-open eyes. "Ah. Ah..."

He protected her. This person. Shido.

He protected her. Miku. A Miku with no voice. A Miku who should have been worthless.

He protected her. He kept that smallest of promises!

She felt something warm in her throat and cried out softly as she unconsciously reached a hand toward Shido.

Her fingers touched his. The body of a boy normally made her want to vomit if she so much as brushed it with her fingertips, but now for some reason, none of that usual revulsion rose up in her.

And then Miku noticed something strange.

Tohka had just attacked them, but now she pressed a hand to her forehead and groaned in anguish. "Unh. Unh... Shido... Shido..."

"...?"

Miku frowned slightly. She was pretty sure that Tohka had just said, "Shido." Was it possible that her memory was coming back?

However.

"Unh. Ah! Aaaaaaaaaaaaah!" Tohka shouted and thrust the tip of Nahemah down into the floor and swung her left hand at the blade.

"Hngh!"

The blade cut into Tohka's palm, bereft of any Astral Dress because of Ellen's attack earlier attack, and she pulled her hand away, bleeding profusely.

With this, Tohka had finally regained her composure.

Although perhaps *regained her composure* wasn't the right way to put it. With bloodshot eyes, Tohka glared at Shido and drew Nahemah wet with her own blood.

"A strange trick...! Do you mean to deceive me, human?!" Tohka said, then kicked at the ground and leaped up into the air again, brandishing her massive sword up high. "Good. In that case, I will turn you to dust with a single blow!"

A mysterious rippling appeared in space, and an enormous throne, twice as tall as Tohka, emerged from the distorted area.

The throne split up into pieces and twisted around the sword Tohka brandished. Shedding black particles with each fragment of the throne that synthesized with it, the massive blade transformed into something even more gargantuan and malevolent.

And when the final piece fused with the sword, the tip thrust up into the sky as if to slice through the moon.

"With my Paverschlev!!" Tohka announced, almost howling.

Nahemah was revealed in its true form.

"That's...!" Shido's eyes flew open wide.

Tohka gripped the hilt of the sword even more tightly. The massive blade began to absorb the particles of black light in the surrounding space.

"...!"

Miku gasped and tried to put up a barrier with her voice. But her Spirit power hadn't recovered to the point where she could use her Angel yet. And even if she had succeeded, she doubted she could have defended against this attack.

"...!"

She couldn't just do nothing and let Shido die. Miku wrapped her arms around him and turned her back to Tohka to protect him.

"Miku?!" Shido cried.

"..., ...!"

But Miku didn't step away.

She couldn't understand her own actions herself.

But vaguely, she felt like she didn't want to let this boy break his promise. She wanted to save Tohka. Yes. She thought this.

That said, however, she could see at a glance the enormity of the Spirit power contained in that sword. Most likely, whatever Tohka had in store for them was an incomparably destructive blow that would devastate everything in view. Miku's small body wouldn't be able to defend against it. She would evaporate together with Shido.

"Begone, human!" Tohka shouted, and brought down the sword shining darkly. The air area creaked and squealed.

However.

"…?!"

At the tip of the sword Tohka swung, Miku felt nothing but the already cool air drop further in temperature.

"Zadkiel…!"

"All right! Okay! Here we go!"

Familiar voices called out, and a current of icy air assaulted Tohka.

"Ngh?" Tohka scowled and put up a wall of Spirit power to offset this attack.

She looked over to Yoshino floating in the air, clinging to the back of a massive stuffed rabbit.

"Tohka…! What is going on…?! Attacking Shido…!"

Miku felt something off in Yoshino's words. And her eyes flew open. When her voice had disappeared, her control had been released.

And.

"…Huh?"

She pulled away from Shido.

His body was radiating heat like a bonfire.

"You… Impudent!"

Holding Paverschlev, Tohka blocked the attack of icy air and wind, and frowned.

Shido gently pulled away from Miku, who had stepped out to protect him.

In his right hand, the shining sword Sandalphon. And in his left, a shield of Zadkiel's icy air.

When Tohka had launched her slicing attack at Miku, the chilled Angel had manifested in his left hand, just like Sandalphon.

"Ah... Unh!" Miku tugged on the hem of his shirt. She was apparently worried about him.

But he had to go. Shido smiled at Miku. "I gotta get going. To rescue the princess. To keep my promise."

"Ah..." Miku quietly released her hand and nodded.

But for Yoshino now, in her limited unlocked state, it was apparently hard for her to hold Tohka. The older Spirit stood strong against Zadkiel's attack, holding Paverschlev tightly. Most likely, in his current state, Shido would be blown away the second he approached her.

But for some reason, he looked up at her with a curiously calm heart.

Maybe it was an effect of the constant use of the Angel—his whole body ached as if it were being torn apart. And as if they were urging this battered body to move, the flames of Ifrit raced through him. He was in such incredible anguish that it should have driven him insane.

But Shido didn't let that stop him. Slowly, but surely, he approached Tohka.

"Tohka." He called her name, and her shoulders jumped up as if she was afraid.

"...!"

She shook her head as though pushing this away and screamed as she brought down the enormous sword.

"Nahemah! Paverschlev!!"

Instantly, Shido's field of vision was dyed black.

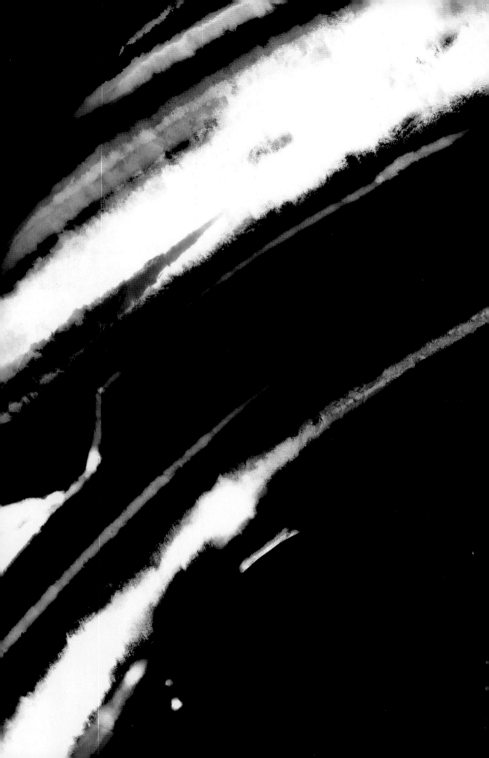

*   *   *

It sounded like the air itself was ripping apart.

A line shot out from the end of Tohka's sword and swallowed everything in its path.

The half-destroyed building. The ground spreading out below it. The town beyond this. And the mountains visible even farther out.

And then a wave of Spirit power rode out along this line and obliterated everything that existed upon it. This was no joke, no metaphor. Everything this current of black Spirit power touched was compressed, smashed, and turned to dust, vanishing on the wind.

"...!"

Slumped down on the floor of the building, Miku kept herself low to the ground so that she wouldn't be blown away by the aftershocks that whipped past her as she gasped.

Through the buildings, the city, the earth, there was a straight path of nothingness.

Yoshino hung in the sky, likely knocked aside from the blowback of Tohka swinging Nahemah. But no matter how she sent her eyes racing around, she could catch no sign of Shido anywhere.

The spot where he had been standing was deeply, deeply gouged out, leaving a spectacular crater.

"...! ...!" Miku cried out almost inaudibly, doing her best to shout Shido's name.

But she got no response. Had he been erased by Paverschlev? Or had he been caught up in the destruction of the building? Whichever it was, Shido wasn't there.

"Heh. Ha-ha! Ha-ha-ha-ha-ha-ha!" Tohka laughed loudly in the sky above. "Gone. Gone. Finally gone. The crafty, treacherous human trying to deceive me!"

Miku gritted her teeth and glared at Tohka with sharp eyes. But then her eyes grew wide as saucers.

"—"

Tohka floated with the moon behind her. But farther up in the sky.

"Hmph. Wherefore do you laugh, servant? Are you not crowing in victory a little too early?"

"Protection. We are quite fond of our foresight; if we might say so ourselves."

Blanketed in a wind generated by Kaguya and Yuzuru, hanging in the sky, was Shido.

A curious sense of buoyancy. He had been transferred a distance of 15,000 meters by the *Fraxinus* transporter and moved at high speeds by the hand of a Spirit, but this was the first time he'd flown through the sky wrapped in a concentrated mass of wind.

The instant Tohka swung Paverschlev, Kaguya and Yuzuru appeared from behind the building and saved Shido. It seemed that they had seen this coming right from the beginning and kept themselves hidden.

"Thanks, you two. You saved me."

"Kah-kah! Pay it no mind. Such a display is a trifling for us."

"Assent. I'm glad that you're okay. Anyway."

"Yeah. Please and thank you."

Kaguya and Yuzuru nodded and made El Re'em and El Na'ash vibrate.

And then they tossed Shido clad in a wind barrier toward Tohka. Actually, it was more like they dropped him on her. Wrapped in wind, Shido fell toward Tohka's head like a ball.

"Wha—" She turned her face up, noticing Shido closing in from above. "You... You're still alive?!"

She released Paverschlev and swung Nahemah.

Maybe she couldn't use the overwhelming power of Paverschlev multiple times in a row. Or maybe she had decided it wasn't to her advantage to focus all that power at this close range. Either way, it didn't change the fact that this would be a lethal blow for Shido.

"Ngh—"

He still had thirty meters to go. Considering the speed of his descent, it wouldn't even take a second to cross this distance.

But that was too slow against an opponent like Tohka. She would swing Nahemah before her reached her and easily cut him in two.

However.

"—Ah."

For some reason, for a mere instant, as she swung Nahemah upward, Tohka stopped.

A strange sensation passed through the Spirit raising the sword above her head.

The moment she saw the human gripping Sandalphon dropping down from above, a fragment of her buried memory exploded into her consciousness.

"I. Have seen this—"

Before.

At the same time that she realized this, the memory—a scene she should have never witnessed before—was projected vividly in her mind.

A Spirit brandishing a massive sword. And a boy screaming her name as he fell from the sky.

Toooooooohkaaaaaaaaaaaaaaaaaaaaaaaaaaaaaaaaaaaaaaaaaaaaaaaaa aaaaaaaaaaaaaaaaaaaaaaaaaaaaaaaaaaaaaaaaaaaaaaaaaaaaaaaaaaaaaa aaaaaa!!

"Toh...ka..."

She digested the name in her memory.

This was indeed the name this human closing in from the sky used to refer to her.

Tohka. Tohka. It was a word she couldn't have heard before. And yet it...

"Ngh..." She felt a sharp pain in her head.

In that instantaneous opening.

"Tohka!" The boy dropping from the sky drew closer. "Hey, Tohka. I came to rescue you."

"You whelp...!" She scowled and clenched her sword tightly. But he was already too close. It was obvious that the boy would pierce her chest with Sandalphon before she could swing. Unconsciously, she gritted her teeth and braced herself for the pain.

But the boy took a totally unexpected action.

The Angel. He released into the air the sole weapon that could have hurt her. And on top of that, at the same time, he dispersed the cold air swirling in his left hand.

Basically, he had left himself completely defenseless before his enemy.

"What are you—"

"If I kept that stuff around…it'd hurt, right?" the boy said, and squeezed her tightly with a somewhat tense look on his face.

Unable to read the boy's intentions, she frowned. "Wha… You—" But she wasn't able to finish her sentence.

The reason was simple. Because the boy had pressed his lips up against hers.

Her head was thrown into turmoil.

What on earth was this boy doing? To an enemy. On the battlefield. A kiss? To what end? To get her to drop her guard? But then why throw the sword away? She didn't understand. Her vision was hazy, her mind in turmoil. *Shido.* Shido? This thing like a name, like a word, flitted through her mind, and the turmoil increased. Her head was spinning. From her buried memories, scattered fragments—*Shido*—began to—*Shido*—pop up. It was almost like—*Shido*—her body was not her—*Shido*—own. This name—*Shido*—ate into her consciousness. Each time this name—*Shido*—echoed, she grew more uncomfortable—*Shido*—but it was somehow not a bad feeling. Why had she—*Shido*—forgotten? *He named me.* His presence—*Shido*—flipped everything upside down…

"Shi…do…?"

Tohka moved her lips and spoke the name of the boy embracing her.

And then the Astral Dress of darkness she was wearing and the sword she held in her hand turned into particles and melted into the air.

But for some reason, she wasn't particularly surprised. Those weren't Tohka's things. It was only natural that she wouldn't be able to wear them.

"Yup," Shido replied briefly, and smiled with relief. And then slumped over. Tohka hurriedly pulled him close to her.

But she needn't have worried. A veil of wind formed around her and Shido to wrap them up and slowly carry them to the ground.

Tohka looked around. At the building with the top floors blown away, at the bisected city. Yoshino and the Yamai sisters were nearby, and Miku was slumped on the ground.

She had no idea what was going on. Shido had been moments away from being killed by Ellen, and the moment Tohka realized she couldn't do anything about it, that she couldn't turn even to her Angel for help, she had lost consciousness.

"Ngh..." An anguished groan from Shido interrupted Tohka's thoughts.

"Sh-Shido! Are you okay?!"

"Yeah... More or less," he said, and managed to stand on his own two feet. But he was battered and bruised, and he looked like he might fall over again at any second. Tohka pulled him to her tightly as if to support him.

"But you, Tohka... Are *you* okay? What exactly *was* that?"

"Huh...? What do you mean?" Tohka asked in reply, her eyes wide.

Shido got a troubled look on his face and then stroked her hair. "Nah... It's fine. We'll leave that stuff to Kotori and Reine. Right now—welcome back, Tohka."

"Mm...? Mm." She cocked her to one side for a second but then nodded firmly. "I'm back... Shido."

As the morning sun began to shine through the bisected city, the two of them saw their shadows overlapping on the floor of the building.

Several shadows wriggled inside the dark, rubble-filled building.

This early in the morning, with the sun having only just risen, and in the middle of a spacequake alarm, there couldn't have been anyone who merely wandered into a place like this. And if someone who knew nothing of all this were to witness this sight, they would suspect it was a hallucination or a dream.

At any rate, the girls there all had exactly the same face.

"The target was not in DEM Building Two."

"The cutting-edge technology laboratory was a miss."

"Only Tohka was in the first building."

Hearing her own voice reporting one after the other, Kurumi sighed with annoyance where she sat on top of the rubble.

"It seems that this place is also not it, hm?"

Even though she had used nearly a thousand avatars, she hadn't gotten any real results. Kurumi shrugged slightly.

"The captive Spirit. Where on earth could you be?" she murmured.

This was what Kurumi was searching for.

The second Spirit to have been sighted in this world. The sole person who could teach her about the primeval Spirit.

Even if she did get to eat Shido with his Spirit power and become able to use the twelfth bullet Yud Bet, it would all be pointless if she couldn't shoot the first Spirit.

Kurumi had offered to work with Shido in order to find this Spirit held captive by DEM Industries, confined in a facility somewhere in the world.

But it seemed that it had been a fool's errand from start to finish.

"Well, we can't do anything about that now. I will simply call today a good one for having gotten Shido to stroke my hair. Right, us?" Kurumi said, and countless Kurumis squirming in the darkness disappeared into her shadow.

Epilogue
After the Festival

Dear Shido Itsuka,

Please come to the greenroom of the central stage at 2:50 PM on the third day of the Tenou Festival. I have something I wish to discuss with you alone. I'll get angry if you don't come!

Your Miku

It was evening of the day of the incident at DEM that such a letter was delivered to Shido, revealing to him a personality so obviously different from the one she'd had up to that point (complete with a kiss on the page).

"What the..." He read the letter in his hand one more time before scratching at the back of his head.

Monday, September 25. The third day of the Tenou Festival and the day after the attack on DEM Industries Japan branch office.

After undergoing a barrage of careful testing for a full day on *Fraxinus*, Shido ventured out to the venue for the Tenou Festival, Tengu Square.

Compared with the first day, there were noticeably fewer people. As there should have been. Right from the start, the third day of the Tenou

Festival had been positioned as a kind of after-party, a day for only the students from the ten participating schools to enjoy the festival.

In the end, the mysterious riot that had happened in Tengu was swept away as a terrorist incident in which a special stimulant had been disseminated.

Shido thought that this was honestly a bit of a stretch. But Miku's believers, who suddenly came back to their senses yesterday morning, had absolutely no memory of being controlled, and so they didn't pursue the truth of the rioting. However illogical it may have been, it was consistent at any rate. The silver lining was that no one had died in all the chaos.

The disastrous scene at DEM Industries Japan branch office, too, was explained away as damage from a special spacequake. There was probably video from the surveillance cameras, but the company wouldn't go out of their way to publicize a battle between Spirits and Wizards.

Kurumi had disappeared at some point after helping Shido. He'd thought she would want something from him in return... But she hadn't shown herself. Not to him anyway.

Looking around the venue, he began to walk slowly.

With all the commotion, the second day of the Tenou Festival had obviously been abruptly canceled, and the opening on the third day had been in danger of the same fate. But because of the enthusiasm of the students and some string pulling behind the scenes by Ratatoskr, the festival had opened that day without incident.

On top of that, the canceled second day was being carried over to tomorrow... Which gave them the slightly mystifying schedule of more school festival following the after-party, but the students didn't really give that too much thought.

"Keh-keh...Shido. Are your wounds healed already? Heh. I'd expect nothing less from a man we have such high hopes for."

"Question. Tohka is still not allowed to come?"

Kaguya and Yuzuru in maid uniforms called out to him when he passed by the maid café.

"Yeah," he said. "They're still not done with the tests. I'll have to bring her a souvenir from the festival."

"Hmm. I suppose so. Then, Shido. For what reason are you in costume as a boy today?"

"Conformity. Yuzuru is also curious. What happened to Shiori?"

"In costume... I *am* a boy!" Shido scowled and shouted, and the Yamai sisters burst out laughing. "Unbelievable."

He told them he'd be back later, waved, and left the maid café behind. Yes. There was something he had to do today.

He slipped past the booths toward the central stage. When he opened the door, a lively song and clapping loud enough to shake the air echoed around him.

Miku was onstage. Wrapped in her Astral Dress, she was singing in that voice imbued with Spirit power that bewitched people. It was no wonder the audience was going wild for her.

The song ended, and Miku bowed, moving her shoulders up and down slightly. The venue exploded into deafening applause.

"Thank you so much, everyone! Really!" she said and then left the stage. There was another round of applause, and he could hear people chanting Miku's name.

He'd never be able to wade through this crowd to reach the other side of the audience seating. Shido left the stage area, went around to the back, and stepped through the staff entrance into a world of clutter.

When he was standing in front of the greenroom door, he knocked.

"Yes, come in!"

He heard a voice from inside call. He took a deep breath and then pushed the door open.

Miku was alone in the greenroom, sitting on a chair. A sports drink bottle was set out next to her, and a towel hung around her neck.

After the incident at DEM, even after Miku got her voice back, she showed no sign of resistance. She very obediently followed the instructions of the Ratatoskr members who came to clean up the mess.

Because there had been no way to seal her Spirit powers as long as Shido was out of commission, all Ratatoskr could do was monitor her. But during that time, they hadn't seen any threatening behaviors. In fact, Miku had even asked them to deliver a letter to Shido. What kind of change had come over her exactly? She was so different, it was like she'd been possessed.

Actually—

"So you came, *daaaarling*!" Miku said brightly, and leaped up from her chair to abruptly embrace Shido.

"D-darling...?!" He was completely baffled. He stared at Miku, who had a childlike carefree smile on her face. "You... What exactly is going on? You hated boys so much, and now you're..."

"Hee-hee-hee! You're special, darling. You saaaved my life," she said, and drew even closer to him. Her ample bosom pressed up against his chest.

"Hey!" He jumped a little.

And maybe she sensed this. The smile on her face changed, like she was toying with him. Her reaction made him think back to when he was in Shiori mode.

Indeed, he'd heard that Miku's mental state had been extremely good since the DEM incident. And that his likability with her had shot up dramatically. But he couldn't believe it was to this extreme.

He'd had this thought before, but her personality and her values really were very close to those of a child. Something that she had hated and hated changed into love at a single stroke. For her, this switch had been the events at DEM.

Smiling wryly, Shido opened his mouth like he'd just remembered something. "So then, Miku. What did you want to talk about?"

"Ohh, thaaat!" Miku nodded. She turned toward Shido in a casual gesture.

And stood on her tiptoes and kissed him.

"...?!"

He darted his eyes around in confusion. But Miku held on to him tightly and didn't take her lips away.

"Mmngh..."

"...Mm!"

While they were kissing, Shido felt something warm flowing into his body. At the same time, the Astral Dress that Miku was wearing turned into particles of light and melted into the air.

"Ah... Eeek!" Miku had noticed this, too. She finally pulled her lips away from his. "Such quick work... D-darling, you're suuuuch a pervert..."

"No! I didn't! It wasn't—"

"Hee-hee-hee! I'm kiiiidding. Yoshino and the others told me. I know everything," she said, smiling, still pressed up against him.

"Huh...?" Shido furrowed his brow. Yoshino and the others told her? She must have meant the true method of locking away Spirit powers.

In other words, Miku had kissed Shido fully aware that it would seal away her Spirit powers.

"Miku, you...," he said, stunned.

After she had been so afraid of losing her voice, why on earth would she...?

Miku parted her small lips. "Because...you promised me."

"Promised you?"

"Yes." She nodded firmly. "You said that even if I lost my voice and everyone turned away from me, you alone would be my fan. That... was true, yes?"

"Ohh..." Shido had indeed said that while they were at DEM's Japan branch. "Of course," he declared, looking into her eyes.

That hadn't been a joke or some kind of flattery. Even Shido, who didn't generally have much interest in idols and that sort of thing, was seriously impressed by Miku's singing.

She grinned, carefree, as she looked up at his face. "You keeeept your promise. If I have you, I'll be okay. I can trust you at least." She squeezed the arms she had wrapped around him. "Even if I lose this voice. Even if no one comes to listen to me sing. As long as you're here, that's enough. If that happens...I'll sing just for you."

"Miku..." Shido pursed his lips and spread his arms to hug Miku back.

But just before he could wrap his arms around her, the door to the greenroom flew open, and a girl wearing the Rindoji Girls' Academy uniform came in.

"Miku! Your encore was too amazing, and they won't let us move on to the next act! Could you do one—Huh?!"

The girl froze, the door still open in her hand.

But that was only natural. The super-popular idol had had her clothes peeled away and was being attacked by a strange man (or so it looked).

"H-help! Heeeeeeelp!"

"Hey! Hold on! You've got the wrong idea!" Shido called to the girl, flustered, and she whirled her eyes around in confusion before turning and running away.

Miku had stared at this, jaw hanging open, but now she began to giggle uncontrollably.

"Ah-ha-ha! Wouldn't it be best if you hurried out of here? They'll catch you if you staaaay, you know?"

"Hey, that ain't funny," Shido said.

Miku laughed again before bringing her face up. "But she did mention something about an encore, didn't she?"

"Huh? Ohh… Yeah."

"Well then, I have to go. As for my costume… Yes, I could ask someone from the maid café to let me borrow a uniform. Will you watch, darling?" Miku asked. Her eyes shone with a serious anxiety and a powerful will that was greater than the anxiety.

"Yup!" Shido nodded firmly.

A spotlight shone on the stage. At once, the voices calling for an encore that filled the venue fell silent.

"Okaaay! We meet again, hm?"

Miku's appearance in a maid uniform was greeted with roaring cheers.

Shido looked up at her from a seat in the audience. He'd managed to flee the greenroom before anyone came, and he entered the stage area through the main entrance, where he waited for Miku to come on.

"Thanks for calling me baaack for an encore! But you really shouldn't have. You're making trouble for the staff," Miku said, the tiniest bit angry, and a cry of "sorry" echoed through the venue.

"But it makes me really haaaappy. So special just for today, I'd like to sing a song that's really important to me."

Miku snapped her fingers, and upbeat music began to play.

Naturally, cheers rose up, but at the same time, Shido could also hear voices whispering and wondering.

Which only made sense. This song was Tsukino Yoimachi's, the song on the CD he'd found at Miku's house.

"This…" Shido gasped and stared at her.

The song in Miku's story. The song she was supposed to sing onstage when she suffered from the voice loss all that time ago.

"—!"

Miku began to sing a song that she hadn't performed in a long time.

The Spirit power that seduced people was no longer present in that voice. He could see a faint confusion on the faces of the audience members at the notable difference.

But as the song progressed, the audience grew as wildly enthusiastic as they had been at the performance two days earlier. To the point where this song got just as much applause and cheering as the one she'd finished before this encore.

The song finally ended, and the stage erupted in loud clapping and cheering.

"…!"

Looking out at the venue, Miku shed tears as she gripped the mic.

"Everyone… Thank. You. So…!"

A murmur ran through the crowd.

However.

"Thank…you…darling… I love you…!"

The crowd erupted at these very significant words uttered out of the blue by the idol, and Shido retreated, a cold sweat running down his face.

Afterword

Hello! Koshi "the subtitle is Miku, but the cover art is not Miku" Tachibana here.

I'm bringing you *Date A Live 7: Truth Miku*. The story has spanned a few volumes, but this is coming to you in the form of opening and closing volumes for the first time, in the sense that the same Spirit name is in the title. How did you like it? I would be delighted if you enjoyed the story.

I believe those of you who read the book understand, but some of the illustrations in this volume are truly incredible. Those of you who haven't read it yet, please do take a look.

I wrote this in the beginning as well, but even though the subtitle for this volume is *Truth Miku*, a different girl decorates the cover. The design is very black, hm? Black in a very nice way.

Which reminds me of a question I've had for a while. Why does the amount of skin exposed increase when a female character goes dark? To touch on the tokusatsu shows and anime from my youth, I suppose it's because the schema of black = bad = sexy lady is imprinted on my brain. Put another way, when the evil woman leader in a suggestive outfit from the start disguises herself to try and trick the hero, I feel like she usually wears something that covers up more skin and adopts a neat and tidy persona. There really must be this and that in there tying a sense of virtue to good and evil, and as for what I'm trying to say here, it's that the belly button on the cover is sexy.

Now then. The anime broadcast is also drawing near. The TV animation *Date A Live* is scheduled to begin broadcasting in April 2013. Please do tune in and watch.

Also, the release date for the *Date A Live* short story collection has been decided. It's full of complementary information on the everyday lives of the characters that doesn't overwrite the story. This will be on sale in May 2013. I hope you'll pick it up.

Once again, this book was put together with the help of so many people.

Tsunako, my editor, everyone else involved in the publication and sale of the book, the many people involved in the anime and media mix. Thank you so much.

All right then. I pray we will meet again.

Koushi Tachibana
February 2013